He took a step into the room. "Do you remember me, Stephanie?" he asked, almost shy.

"Certainly. Connor Riley, wide receiver for the New Orleans Sinners, last seen through my viewfinder yesterday with thirty seconds to play in the game. Your team did win?" she asked, trying to put him at ease.

Of the three, he seemed the most stricken about her condition, but then, he was the one who had landed directly on her and put that helmet-sized bruise on her chest. Thank heaven, her legs had splayed open, or both of them might have been broken.

"Sure did. Ancient Andy came through for us again," Billodeaux answered for the tongue-tied Riley.

"Do you remember Kevin Riley?" Connor hinted.

"Of course, the first of my lying, cheating boyfriends. See, no brain damage from the fall," Stevie answered glibly. Then, she put a hand to her mouth and took it away again. "Oh, no! You're Kevin's little brother. All this time following the Sinners and I never tied the names together. I guess I put everything to do with him out of my mind. We played football together once when you were just a high school kid."

Connor sidled up to the bed, seized the only chair and presented his bouquet. "You said you liked daisies because they were simple and cheerful."

"You remembered that? We only met the one time when he brought me home to meet your parents, but they were out of town. Your brother dumped me the next weekend because we'd dated three months and I hadn't put out for him. But you remembered I liked daisies?"

Goals for a Sinner

by

Lynn Shurr

This is a work of fiction. Names, characters, places, and incidents either are the product of the author's imagination or are used fictitiously, and any resemblance to actual persons living or dead, business establishments, events, or locales, is entirely coincidental.

Goals for a Sinner

Contact Information: info@thewildrosepress.com

Cover Art by *Angela Anderson*

The Wild Rose Press
PO Box 708
Adams Basin, NY 14410-0706
Visit us at www.thewildrosepress.com

Publishing History
First Champagne Rose Edition, 2010
Print ISBN 1-60154-717-X

Published in the United States of America

Dedication

For my husband, Dave, who answered questions even when the game was on and serves faithfully as my computer geek.

Chapter One

With the weight of her long blonde ponytail streaming out behind her through the loop in her black New Orleans Sinners football cap, Stevie Dowd raced down the sidelines toward the end zone. She stumbled to a stop, turned, braced her legs and raised the Canon EOS digital camera to her eye. This was it—her chance at the cover of *Sports Illustrated* magazine. No more being assigned to photograph rhythmic gymnastics or water ballet. No more being razzed by the guys about her "sensitive" portrait of the little lame bat boy. Stevie Dowd was in the right place at the right time.

The long pass thrown by reserve quarterback Joe Dean Billodeaux sailed down the field past the other photographers jostling each other at the fifty yard line. The football seemed to spin out on an endless trajectory. Then, just as Stevie had bet, wide receiver Connor Riley charged down the field in a race to get under the ball. His calf muscles bunched under the tight leggings of the Sinner's all-black uniform. His arms reached skyward. "Let him fill the frame," Stevie schooled herself with time-honored advice.

Riley was so close now she could see his signature blond curls sticking out from under his helmet and resting on his shoulder pads. He turned his head to search for the ball and the red devils on his helmet seemed to wink at Stevie as she pressed the shutter at the very moment he leapt and connected with the pigskin. She captured him going up and coming down with the prize. As the wideout touched ground and dug in to take a step toward the goal line ten yards away, Falcon cornerback, Revelation "Rev" Bullock, rose up behind him, a black mountain all covered in white, and came crashing down on Riley like a two-hundred pound avalanche. Stevie surged forward and kept rapid fire snapping.

The two men locked together arrowed out of bounds and Stevie Dowd caught every nuance of it with her camera. She took one more step closer and was buried beneath four hundred pounds of football player.

The Rev removed his massive frame from his opponent's torso and offered a hand to Connor Riley, who shook his head as he rose. That was the Rev for you, always the good sport, but something felt wrong. He had landed on a surface much softer than artificial turf.

The Rev spit out his mouth guard. "Couldn't let you get away from me and score, man, but it looks like we done sacked ourselves a photographer and he out cold."

"She," corrected Riley, noticing the blonde ponytail fanned out behind the delicate head of an unconscious woman. The hair held the black Sinners cap in place despite the impact. She had made no attempt to save herself. Both her arms protected a fancy digital camera held to one side away from the blow. She was fair, probably paler than usual now, no makeup, and no color on her partially open pink lips. Her long, light brown lashes fluttered as if she were getting ready to wake from her bed after a long, steamy night of sex.

Riley shook his head again. This celibacy thing was getting to him. Thank God the season was nearly over. Still, he remembered something about this woman, something familiar that didn't come to him. The medics interrupted his thoughts as they squeezed between the two players and knelt by the victim whose feet lay splayed open on the playing field. The short, balding medic unsnapped the many-pocketed photographer's vest. Riley inhaled.

She wore nothing under the vest but a white Sinners T-shirt with its little red devil logo plastered by sweat against one full, braless breast. Her nipples were clearly delineated and peaked up in the cool stadium air. Riley swallowed his saliva.

The Rev elbowed him. "You lusting after a knocked out woman, brother."

"I know, I know," Riley confessed. "This was all your idea."

"Best season you ever had, right?" the Rev answered.

"I know," Riley said again. "But there's something else about her."

The medics listened to the patient's chest, checked her blood pressure. When her big blue eyes opened, the EMT with the crew cut held up two fingers and asked her "how many."

"Ah, four. No, two. Three?" she answered faintly, trying to cooperate.

"She's guessing. Concussion. Do you know your name?" The balding medic spoke slowly and clearly.

"Ah—" was the only answer that came from the full pink lips.

The other medic checked her credentials. "Says her name is Stevie Dowd." He wrote on the chart he held.

"Not hardly a dowd," the Rev commented.

"Not Stevie, either," Connor Riley said. "It's Stephanie, Stephanie Dowd, my brother's old girlfriend, the woman I loved my entire senior year of high school."

"Get out." The Rev pounded Connor on the back. "A lost love. Good things come to those who wait. Didn't I just tell you?"

Stevie's pink lips moved again trying to articulate a whole sentence. Connor removed his helmet and walked around the medics to kneel by her side. “Stephanie, it’s Connor. What can I do for you?” he asked.

“My pictures. *Sports Illustrated.* Get them to—” Her eyes closed again.

Riley looked up suddenly aware of the click and whir of other cameras around him. He pointed to one of the sports photographers preserving the moment on a memory card. “You, Dexter Sykes,” he commanded, reading the name off the man’s ID. “See that this camera gets to *Sports Illustrated.* And I better not see your name on the photo credits.”

Gently, Riley unfolded Stevie’s hands off of her Canon. He unfastened the neck strap and thrust the whole piece of equipment at the man he had selected from the group. “See she gets her camera back, too,” he added with just the faintest threat.

“Sure thing, Mr. Riley. We all know Stevie. She’s been trying to get a shot like this for years. How about one for me, Connor?”

The photographer snapped without waiting for an answer. Connor blinked and gave a low growl. Dexter Sykes stepped back behind the other photographers and took off at a run, rushing the pictures to *Sports Illustrated,* no doubt.

The emergency cart arrived. The medics secured her head and neck, slid a board under Stevie and strapped her down. On a count of three, they raised the board and placed her on the cart for the run to the waiting ambulance. Connor Riley watched Stephanie Dowd move out of his life again, this time on the Sinners’ meat wagon.

****

In the broadcasting booth, once the commercials had run, sportscasters Al Harney and Hank Wilkes filled the dead air time with their patter.

“For those who are just joining us, we are experiencing a delay of game. An innocent civilian got in the way of the troops and was mowed down by wide receiver, Connor Riley, and cornerback Rev Bullock at the end of the most spectacular play of the game. The medics are checking out the victim now and the game will resume once they get the meat wagon off the field. Say, Al, do you remember the time back in '96 a cameraman got sacked?"

"I do, Hank. That one always makes funniest sports videos. Here's another one for the show. But about that play, Billodeaux's long pass set a new record for the Super Dome and for this relatively young expansion team, the New Orleans Sinners, who moved in here when the Saints were lured to Salt Lake to take up residence in a new stadium near the Jazz. I wonder how happy the Saints players are because I can tell you Temple Avenue ain't no Bourbon Street. The Sinners are doing their best to fill the gap left by the Saints though."

"Yes, they have quite a reputation, but that doesn't seem to be hurting their play any this year. The next thirty seconds of the game will determine which of these teams goes on to win the wild card spot in the coming playoffs. The score is twenty-one to twenty with the Falcons in the lead. Three touchdowns to the Sinners' two and two field goals and thanks to Billodeaux's long pass, the Sinners are now within easy field goal range again."

"Give some credit to wideout, Connor Riley. This is a case of the receiver making the quarterback look good, Hank. Riley is the only man on the Sinners' team with the speed to get under a pass overthrown by a mile on the third down. Billodeaux has an arm, but not much control. The loss of veteran quarterback, Art Golden, with a broken leg at the beginning of the third quarter is going to hurt the Sinners in the playoffs unless Billodeaux settles down. But, the boy has potential. Could be Art might get his only Super Bowl ring sitting on the bench after playing out his last years on this young team."

"There's the whistle, Al. As the meat wagon goes

into the tunnel, the Sinners' field goal team takes the field. Ancient Andy Mortenson gets into position, kicks, and it's good. At forty-two, he's still got the toe. The Sinners go on to the playoffs."

Chapter Two

The night had been hellish. Every few hours, a nurse entered her room and nudged Stevie awake to the terrible pain of her concussion. Then, she would ask her patient some idiotic question like, “Do you know where you are, dear?”

“Hospital. Pain,” Stevie would answer.

“We’ll be able to give you something for that in the morning if the doctor okays it. Now go back to sleep.”

Just about the time Stevie slept again, the routine started all over.

In the morning, an orderly brought a breakfast tray. The glassy eye of a poached egg in a cup made her stomach roil, but she did choke down the toast, a cup of hot tea and a few spoonfuls of orange Jell-O guided to her mouth with a shaking hand.

As a reward for her good behavior, an Indian doctor with slick black hair and a wide, white smile prescribed a mild painkiller which allowed Stevie to turn her head very slowly from side to side without the sensation that her brains were oozing out through her nose. She dozed.

When she woke, Stevie found she could focus her eyes again. One worry out of the way. Carefully, she pulled out the front of her hospital gown and peered down into the aperture. A large bruise about the size of a football helmet had formed in the center of her chest. The inner sides of both breasts were prune purple. Below them, the white bandages holding her broken ribs in place covered her torso to the waist. The bruise seemed to continue beyond the bandages, but it was dark down there and hard to tell. The Indian doctor had said she was very, very lucky her lungs had not been punctured or worse internal damage done.

"Those football players, they are like bulldozers," he claimed.

Stevie thought the sensation more like being hit by a fast moving SUV and then run over by an eighteen-wheeler coming from the other direction.

Around one, the flowers and guests began arriving. The Sinners' organization sent three dozen red roses in an enormous black vase that took up most of the space on her windowsill. A stuffed toy red devil was attached to its base with a red bow. A small, white winter bouquet made up mostly of spider mums and glittering curlicue thingamabobs held a card reading, "I'll get your camera back to you, baby. Dex."

She started to shake her head—no-no-no, this could not be happening again—but the inside of her head collided with her skull and forced her to stop. Up until that moment, her worst fear had been that her Canon, ripped from her hands by the impact, was now in the possession of some groundskeeper who had found it after the game and thrown out the memory card. Stevie had just learned there were worse fears than her worst fears. No-good Dex had access to her shots.

The rest of the flowers came delivered in person. A flustered day nurse preceded them. She handed Stevie a disposable comb and a warm washcloth. "You might want to clean up a little. Three of the biggest men I have ever seen are asking to see you. I tell you, that is some prime, grade-A beef on the hoof out there at the nurses' station. Sinners players," she added as if Stevie might not get the drift of the conversation.

"My vest. Is it in the closet?" Stevie asked in a panic. "There's lipstick and some mascara and blush in the top right pocket."

The nurse pulled the vest out on a hanger. She helped Stevie wobble into the bathroom. The little plastic container of blush was cracked and its contents scattered, but Stevie managed to brush up a little color for her cheeks. When she missed her eyelid with the mascara wand and drew a row of lines down her cheek, the good nurse darkened her lashes for her. The eyebrow pencil was broken in two, but the tip still worked well enough. Stevie added some frosty pink lipstick, combed her hair back and secured it with a blue scrunchie from another pocket in the vest.

"How do I look?" she asked the nurse.

"As good as you are going to. Might want to use the potty while you're in here. Let me check for blood before you flush."

Stevie obeyed and hobbled back to bed. As the last sounds of the flush died away, the room filled with Sinners bearing gifts. She recognized Joe Dean Billodeaux, a Cajun quarterback who hadn't played much but had a way with the ladies that kept him in the gossip columns regularly. He was the smallest of the three—if a man over six feet tall and weighing one-ninety could be considered small. He had well-developed shoulders, slim hips, a killer smile, and one red rose which he added to the enormous bouquet on the windowsill.

"*Comment ca va, cher*?" he asked.

"*Tres bien, merci. Et vous*?" The opening dialog of her high school French class came back in an instant. She hoped he wouldn't continue in that language because otherwise, she drew a blank.

"Why, I'm just great, and you don't look so bad yourself for someone who's been tackled by the Rev. You know, Billodeaux means 'love letter' in my language." He leaned amorously over Stevie's bed.

The enormous black man hulking behind Joe Dean elbowed him aside. "Get out wit' your Cajun crap. Let a man apologize for putting this pretty lady in the hospital."

The Rev knew what women wanted. He offered a two-layer box of Godiva chocolates and placed it on her nightstand. The man was both wide and tall. A small, solid gut sat atop thighs the size of telephone poles and when a smile spread across his deep brown face, his head and neck seemed even larger.

Several inches taller than the Rev at a good six-five, the unmistakable Connor Riley hung back in the doorway. He gripped a small bouquet of daisies in front of the large chest that could push through a defensive line in order to gain the open space where his long legs would take him far beyond the meanest blockers. He'd brushed his golden hair back behind his ears. The long ends curled up on his wide shoulders. Connor was the only one of the group not smiling. He took a step into the room. "Do you remember me, Stephanie?" he asked, almost shy.

"Certainly. Connor Riley, wide receiver for the New Orleans Sinners, last seen through my view finder yesterday with thirty seconds to play in the game. Your team did win?" she asked, trying to put him at ease.

Of the three, he seemed the most stricken about her condition, but then, he was the one who had landed directly on her and put that helmet-sized bruise on her chest. Thank heaven, her legs had splayed open, or both of them might have been broken.

"Sure did. Ancient Andy came through for us again," Billodeaux answered for the tongue-tied Riley.

"Do you remember Kevin Riley?" Connor hinted.

"Of course, the first of my lying, cheating boyfriends. See, no brain damage from the fall," Stevie answered glibly. Then, she put a hand to her mouth and took it away again. "Oh, no! You're Kevin's little brother. All this time following the

Sinners and I never tied the names together. I guess I put everything to do with him out of my mind. We played football together once when you were just a high school kid."

Connor sidled up to the bed, seized the only chair and presented his bouquet. "You said you liked daisies because they were simple and cheerful."

"You remembered that? We only met the one time when he brought me home to meet your parents, but they were out of town. Your brother dumped me the next weekend because we'd dated three months and I hadn't put out for him. But you remembered I liked daisies?" Stevie took the flowers and gave Connor a friendly smile.

"You were the most beautiful, most fun, most talented girl Kevin ever brought home, and he went back to Merrilee even though she cheated on him. I sacked you into a pile of leaves that afternoon."

"I shoved pecan leaves down your shirt. We were supposed to be playing touch football."

It was all coming back to her now—a lovely home on Lake Pontchartrain with a big wooded lot and an open area to play football, the rewards Kevin's father earned with his engineering company building bridges and bypasses across the Louisiana swamps. Kevin was supposed to get his degree in the same field and join the business. Stevie supposed he had. She knew he'd married Merrilee the following spring just before graduation.

"So how is Kevin doing?"

"Married, works with my dad, has four kids," Connor recited.

Obviously, he did not want to talk about Kevin. His brother had lured her to the house knowing his parents were away visiting an Aunt Helga who was recovering from surgery. The little brother who had decided to stay home put a snag in the planned seduction. Instead, they played touch football, ordered pizza, and watched a video. And so, she never did sleep with Connor's brother.

"Oh my, four children, and Kevin only thirty."

"The big family was Merrilee's idea. They got an early start. She knows how to hang on to a man."

"Well, I'm glad someone knew how to hang on to Kevin. Would you pour me a glass of water?"

"Sure." Connor's hand shook as he poured from the squat pink plastic pitcher on the bedside table. Water dribbled from the bottom of the cup as he held it out for her and made splotches down the front of her white hospital gown. He pulled a wad of tissue from a handy box and was about to swab Stevie's chest, but she waved him away.

"Bruised, very bruised, don't touch. It will dry."

"Do you want me to hold the cup while you drink?" Connor asked.

"No." Stevie poked the bouquet of daisies into the water and set them by the Godiva chocolates. "Another thing I like about daisies is they are tough and long-lasting, but even daisies need water."

Connor nodded as if she had said something very profound. "Where have you been all these years, Stephanie?"

At the foot of the bed, Joe Dean shifted uneasily and exchanged looks with the Rev. The man might as well have said, "Where have you been all my life?" It was an old pickup line, but said in that tone of voice, might have been a proposal rather than a proposition. Stevie ignored the glance and pretended to miss the point. Men, they just had to try.

"Let's see. After Kevin, I did my senior year abroad in Italy. I liked it so much over there I stayed on for graduate work. I was doing serious black and whites of wrinkled old women and coloreds of the Tuscan landscape—nothing too original. Then, Marcello suggested we go to see the horse races in Siena, a once a year, no-holds-barred event. That was the first time I covered a sport."

Speaking enthusiastically about her profession,

Stevie continued. "There was something about getting a split second shot at a critical moment that grabbed me. I sold a few of those pictures then started going to soccer games, bicycle races, anywhere action could be captured."

Connor said, "Marcello?"

"This guy I lived with for a year or so. Anyhow, I came back to the States with a nice sports portfolio, but found out it was quite a boy's club—very hard for a woman to get a start. I got a few assignments to cover women's sports, gymnastics, golf, that kind of thing, but never the big three, football, basketball, or baseball, unless I was willing to do it on spec. Finally, finally…I get in on the ground to photograph the Sinners and I wind up in the hospital, thanks to my own carelessness." She shrugged, then winced as her broken ribs shifted. "Would any of you happen to know what became of my camera? There were some surefire cover shots in it."

"No worries. I gave it to one of the press people named Dexter Sykes and told him to get it to *Sports Illustrated* just the way you wanted. I said it better be your name on any shots they used or else he could deal with me." Connor patted her hand.

"Ah, thanks, Connor. I was a little worried. Dex and I have a history, a bad history. He sent me a note saying he had my camera. I wasn't sure if it was a nasty joke or the truth, but you've eased my mind. Dex wouldn't cross anyone as big as you. Hell, he probably wouldn't cross me again. I blacked his eye just before I threw him out."

"You and Dexter have…been together, Stephanie?"

"Yes, I have no talent for finding honest men or keeping them. Okay? And about this Stephanie business: I have hated that name since the day I was born, and Steffie is even worse. Please call me Stevie. All the guys do."

"Okay, Stevie, then." But Connor's expression was one of sorrow, as if he had a hard time thinking of her by any other name than Stephanie after all these years.

Joe Dean stirred with impatience like the hyperactive child he had once been. "Say Con, we ought to let Stevie get some rest and go and visit old Artie. He's somewhere in this building, too. I need to see how he's doing."

"I suspect your motives, Joe. How about we pass through the children's ward and spread a little sunshine while we're here," the Rev suggested in his deep preacher's voice.

"Sure." Connor Riley pushed reluctantly out of the room's single chair. "I'll come back to see you, Stephanie, ah…Stevie."

"Don't worry about me. I'm as tough as these daisies."

"And just as sweet and pretty, too."

She laughed, shook her head "no" and instantly regretted the motion. "Go," she said.

On their way out, the three big men collided with a stocky fireplug of a woman bearing a large white teddy bear. She gave them a slight nod as they stepped aside and lit up with a big grin when she saw Stevie.

"Stevie, baby doll, what have men done to you now?"

"Jackie! How did you know?"

Stevie watched the guys stop to listen in on their conversation. Joe Dean must've placed Stevie's guest first because he said, "Jackie Haile, Ladies Professional Golf Tour, top money winner this year."

The Rev jabbed at Joe Dean with an elbow and Stevie almost laughed. "You follow women's golf, do you? Kills the time while you warm the bench?"

"Rev, I take an interest in women, even the ones not likely to be interested in me," the second-string quarterback retorted.

Jackie Haile, a blush pinking her cheeks, closed the door and sat in the chair. She snuggled the teddy bear under the covers next to Stevie. "Here's someone to keep you company in bed since you won't have none of me."

"Stop it, Jackie. You're a great friend, but that's all. Live with it. Now tell me how you got here."

"I was doing a charity tournament sponsored by one of the casinos down in Biloxi. Not a bad gig, great room, wonderful food, big-name entertainment as they say. I was having a cold one in the bar after my round, watching the Sinners' game, and saw you get sacked. Knew it was you by the blonde ponytail flying up in the air even before they announced your name in the replays. Figured that must have hurt. So, I called around to a couple of New Orleans hospitals. When we got rained out, I rented a car, and here I am to cheer you up in your time of need."

"Thanks for coming, but what I really need is another painkiller for this head. See if you can get a nurse for me. I buzzed a while ago."

Jackie strode off into the hall to strong-arm a passing nurse into the room. None too happy about the abduction, the nurse read Stevie's chart. "Sorry, Miss Dowd, you'll have to wait another half hour for medication. I'll be back then."

Stevie remembered not to shrug and instead, gritted her teeth.

"Poor baby doll. Leave it to a pack of oversized boys to mess up the one photographer who ever took a pretty picture of me," Jackie said sympathetically.

"It wasn't a pretty picture. It showed your powerful swing. It showed your power as a woman," Stevie declared.

"And the head shot showed my beautiful ears. No one but you ever noticed my ears. I think they are my best feature." Jackie Haile smoothed back her close-cropped dark hair. Tiny gold hoops pierced the lobes of each of the small, nicely formed ears lying close to her head. "I tell you, you are wasting yourself on men. Come over to the other side for some real lovin', Stevie."

"There hasn't been a man in my life for more than a year. Speaking of which, Connor Riley gave my camera to Dexter Sykes to take care of it for me."

"Why didn't he just stamp on it with his big feet?" Jackie answered, knowing Stevie's history with Dex. "Want me to beat up Sykes for you?"

"That's the second offer I've had today. I can do my own fighting. I just hope any shots he submits end up with my name on them. The last time he sent in my photos, he got the credit line and offered to share the check with me."

"And you blacked his eye and made him sign the check over to you, but I never did see your name on that cover of Smokey LeBlanc hitting the game-winning homer."

"Dex claimed it was a labeling accident. They printed a tiny correction in the next issue, but I'm not sure anyone noticed. My past keeps repeating itself. Guess who Connor Riley is?"

"Lying, cheating Marcello's American cousin?" Jackie guessed.

"Nope. Kevin the Rat's brother. I met him once when he was seventeen and didn't even recall his name. Can you believe he remembered I liked daisies? That was ten years ago."

"Brought these, did he?" Jackie flicked the flowers with the short-cut unpolished nails of her thick fingers. "Sounds like a schoolboy crush to me."

"I hope not. There is no way I want to be mixed up with Kevin Riley's family again. Besides, I've given up on men. And I'm not ready to take up women," Stevie added. Jackie grinned at her.

****

Connor, Joe Dean, and the Rev passed through the children's ward autographing anything held out to them—paper napkins, coloring books, stuffed toys—and high-fiving hands so small and weak their slaps could barely be felt on the calloused palms of the athletes.

"Seeing little kids with IV's in their arms and maybe dying depresses the hell out of me." Joe Dean Billodeaux sighed as they rode the elevator up to Art Golden's suite.

Connor nodded. Sure as hell awful. What sort of world was it where little kids were required to endure so much?

"It's a blessing for your soul, brother. Makes you appreciate what the Lord gave you when you was a child—good health and good parents. From what I hear about your escapades, Joe Dean, you better be scoring a few points in heaven," the Rev answered.

"I wish you'd just retire and take over your daddy's church like you always say you're going to do," Joe Dean sulked. "Don't you think it's time he hung up his pads and followed his calling, Con? A lot of good would come from it. A much weaker Falcons defensive team for one thing. Right?"

Connor Riley was not following their banter. "You don't really think Stephanie is a lesbian, do you?"

"Hell, no. She mentioned relationships with three men in the half hour we were in her room. Of course, she could swing both ways. Her and Jackie Haile, all sweaty, and doing it in a sand trap. That has its possibilities. I might have to check out our Stevie after she mends."

Connor gave Joe Dean an ungentle elbow in the ribs. "She's not your Stevie."

"Hey, I'm still bruised there from the game. Doesn't sound like Stevie Dowd has been saving her virginity for you the last ten years, Con. She must be pushing thirty, too. The age thing makes them desperate. As far as I'm concerned, Stevie is a loose ball that anyone can jump on."

"Stevie is twenty-nine. Her birthday is in

November and mine is in February, so that makes her just two and a quarter years older than me, and she will never be desperate enough to sleep with you!"

Connor slammed the quarterback against the elevator's control panel. The lights for several floors lit up, and the elevator slid to a stop three floors short of their goal. The door opened. A pretty student nurse with red curls bobbing stepped inside.

Joe Dean slipped out of Connor's grasp and gave her his best smile. "Sugar, you sure are going to be the most beautiful nurse on this floor one of these days."

The Rev stepped between Joe Dean and the blushing student nurse. "Get your mind out of the gutter, Joe. We need to talk about celibacy."

"Not having any, thanks. Or rather, I'm getting plenty and would like some more." Joe peered around the Rev at the student nurse who scurried out when the elevator door opened again. "Guess I scared her."

"I expect you to be a gentleman about this. Connor here has an interest in Miss Stevie. You let him court her. If she turns him down, then you get a chance, understood?"

"Court her? Count me out." Billodeaux waited, tapping his foot for the doors to open on their floor. Connor Riley relaxed.

In Art Golden's hospital suite, a black vase of red roses—identical to the one in Stevie's room—sent by the Sinners' management adorned the coffee table. The quarterback's right leg hung strung up in traction and at the other end from the wires and pulleys, Art's weathered face looked up at the ceiling from its nest of pillows. He lay in his own blue silk pajamas, shorties to accommodate his cast. The bump from a previous break of his collarbone protruded at the V neckline of his top, and the scars from elbow surgery showed just below his right sleeve. He looked none too happy to see Joe Dean come into view. "Guess you guys heard the news already," he said, looking miserable.

"We've been in the hospital most of the afternoon visiting the photographer I sacked and the children's ward," Connor told him.

"Looks like my football days are over. The doctors tell me if I smash this leg up again, I could lose it or walk with a permanent limp for the rest of my life. Brenda is happy at last. She's been mad ever since the Cowboys released me and I signed that three-year deal with the Sinners. Wouldn't move here to the Big Easy. She stays on the ranch with the kids. Says it's a healthier environment and when I am ready to admit that thirty-eight is too old to play pro ball, she'll put out the welcome mat. I guess my wife got her wish."

"There will be life after football, Art," the Rev said as if he were visiting a hospice.

"Yeah, I should spend more time with my boys. Daniel's got a good arm, and Austin has speed. Guess you got your wish, too, Billodeaux. You'll be the one taking the team to the playoffs. Hope you make it past the first game," said Art without enthusiasm.

"Connor and me have that all worked out. I pass. He catches. Easy," Joe Dean joked.

"Look, I saw the replays on the news. You were gambling Riley would be there when the ball came down 'cause he wasn't anywhere in the area when you threw that pass. That's a dangerous thing to do in the playoffs."

"But it worked this time and we had nothing to lose but the game if I didn't try."

"I'm saying you better work on your short passes and try running a few yourself or you'll end up getting Connor hurt if you go to him too often. Just take the advice from the old war horse and say thank you."

"*Merci beaucoup*, then," Joe Dean answered giving him a punch on the bicep.

"So, what now?" Connor asked trying to take conversation in another direction.

"Oh, some ranching. I raise quarter horses for a hobby. I've always wanted to open up a barbecue place. Free meals for any of my old teammates. You know, the usual thing washed-up football players do."

"You are done playing, not washed-up," counseled the Rev.

"Never made it to the Super Bowl. Got no ring to show for it," Art Golden said with real regret.

"You're still on the team, and me and Riley are going to get you that ring for sure," Joe Dean swore.

Art gave his visitors a melancholy smile. "I guess it will be easier than doing it myself."

Chapter Three

The Rev cautioned Connor to be careful what he wished for, not to get too greedy with God's blessings. But, what was wrong with wanting it all? He and Joe Dean could win the Super Bowl even from the wild card spot in the playoffs, he was sure. Then, Art Golden could retire with a ring and some dignity. Brenda Golden would be thrilled to have him home permanently. Joe Dean Billodeaux was a little wild, sure, but he'd settle down as the starting quarterback for the New Orleans Sinners. Stevie Dowd's picture of the spectacular catch made the cover of *Sports Illustrated,* complete with her photo credit. He'd made that possible, and it gave him an opening with the woman he had been looking for the past ten years.

Connor brought Stevie a stack of magazines bearing her cover shot. He hefted the bundle still bound by plastic strapping as easily as if he were swinging a lunch bucket. He caught her admiring his biceps before she thanked him for going to the trouble.

"No trouble. I bought out the first newsstand I passed on my way over here. I kept the loose ones. My mom and Aunt Helga will want to frame it. You know how moms are."

"Sort of. My mother doesn't approve of my lifestyle. I think footloose and Bohemian are two of her favorite words when describing me. Maybe I'll have the photo laminated and send it to her anyhow. A *Sports Illustrated* cover may not be another grandchild, but it is big deal to me."

"My mom still has my Peewee football trophies. I guess each family is different. Anyhow, we heard you were getting out and came to take you home."

Stevie looked up from where she had been sitting fully dressed in the clothes she had worn to the game and awaiting the doctor's permission to go home for the past hour. The Rev dwarfed a wheelchair in the hallway while Joe Dean flirted with a nurse.

"Do you guys always hang together?"

"Well, the Rev's season is over and he lives just up the bayou. Joe comes from the same place, but keeps an apartment in the city. He follows us older guys around like the hound he is."

"Hey, I heard that," Joe Dean replied without breaking eye contact with the nurse.

The Indian doctor cleared his throat from behind the wall of men and they got out of the way for his entry. He signed off on Stevie's release, cautioned her to take it easy for the next six weeks and to come in if she experienced any problems. He disappeared in under five minutes.

"Here." Connor heaved the bundle of magazines toward the Rev who caught it close to his chest and tucked it under an arm. Joe Dean brought the chair up to the bed, scuffled with Connor for possession, and then stepped back as Riley helped Stevie into her ride to the front door. "Joe, how about bringing the flowers?"

The quarterback cradled the large black vase with his throwing arm and snagged the daisies and Dex's tribute with the other arm. He managed to break off one of the roses and pass it to the nurse on his way out. "I'll call you, sugar."

"Oh, yes," Joe Dean muttered on the way down the hall in the wheelchair's wake. "I do love nurses. They know their way around the human body." They all ignored him.

In the lobby, Stevie asked if the players would

call a cab. "A friend drove my car home from the Dome parking lot. I rent an old house over near the racetrack where they hold the Jazz Festival. You wouldn't believe the rent I pay for that ramshackle place, but hey, it survived Hurricane Katrina. I have enough space for a darkroom, a studio, and an office on the first floor with the kitchen, and a bedroom, bath, and sitting room upstairs. I can pull my car around the back and lock the gate...so it has some good points. Being able to walk to the Jazz Festival is another."

"You have a ride. The Rev has gone to get his SUV from the garage. Is there anyone home to stay with you?" It seemed like a natural question to ask, Connor thought.

"No, my mother is in Houston. She's afraid of flying and doesn't like long drives, but I guess she would have come if I asked her. She moved to be near her grandchildren after my dad passed away a few years ago. My sister has two girls and is married to a pharmacist there. Dex and I shared my place for a while until we had this misunderstanding about one of my pictures. Funny, I missed the extra rent money more than Dex."

"That's good," said Connor as the Rev's mammoth black Cadillac Escalade pulled up under the canopy. "I mean, that's not good—for you to stay alone when you're injured."

"I'm fine, just a little creaky. The headache is nearly gone. My bruises are turning yellow around the edges and my ribs are okay as long as I don't take a deep breath."

"Still..." Connor insisted as he helped her up into the front seat and snapped her seatbelt into place.

"I'm used to taking care of myself, thanks."

The Rev followed Stevie's directions and maneuvered through the lethal New Orleans traffic without swearing once. They pulled up in front of

Stevie's place. Her house had a certain charm with its peeling pale yellow paint and dark green louvers over the windows. A flight of twelve worn wooden steps and two wobbling cast iron handrails with an acorn pattern led up to a small porch raised well above the flood level for that part of town. A window air conditioner hung over the alley running along side of the house to the parking area gated with the same oak leaf and acorn patterned wrought iron. She stood at the bottom of the steps, denied herself a deep breath and started to ascend.

Suddenly, she was flying through the air, a bit like she had at the Sinners' game, but painlessly. Connor Riley, careful of her ribs, scooped her into his arms and carried her toward the door. Billodeaux followed like the flower girl at a wedding. The Rev set his car alarm and pounded after them. The aged stairs trembled beneath their weight.

"Ah, that was exciting and unexpected," Stevie said.

"Really?" Connor answered, looking pleased with himself.

"You can put me down. I'm no light weight, I know."

"I can handle you."

"Connor, I have to get my keys out now."

Stevie slithered down his front and dug in her vest for the keys. She opened two deadbolts and the regular door lock and invited the group inside where another tall, dark staircase to the second floor dominated the hall.

On the left sat her studio filled with lights and drapes, a worktable holding her mat cutter and a clutter of frames. On the right, a small office held a good computer and an excellent printer/scanner. Another door led to her darkroom. A fifties-era kitchen filled the back of the house.

"You need to go upstairs and rest," Connor insisted.

"Don't even think about carrying me. One slip and every Sinners' fan will hate me like they despise the guy at the Cubs game who reached out for a ball and blew their chances for a World Series."

Stevie edged up the steps with the three men following her. Immediately she became embarrassed by the unmade bed and the abandoned lunch dishes on a coffee table in front of the television in the sitting room. None of the guys seemed to notice her less than great housekeeping. The men looked at her photographs decorating every wall—sepia shots of the horserace in Siena, a *Sports Illustrated* cover of a baseball player, a series on Jackie Haile, the golfer—whatever Stevie was proud enough of to put into a frame.

"Nice work," said the Rev. "Very nice work. There's a good one of me taking Connor down on the inside of the magazine. I look ferocious. That's good for my image."

The Rev stretched the plastic bands on the magazine bundle and pulled a copy from the stack. "See here." He flipped the pages. "You can almost hear the bones crack. Oh, sorry."

A small inset showed Stevie buried beneath Connor and the Rev. The credit line belonged to Dexter Sykes, as did the one shot of Joe Dean Billodeaux throwing the pass Connor caught on the cover. Somehow, Dex always managed to profit from her work.

Joe Dean looked over the Rev's shoulder. "Nice one of me, too. I sure am glad I wasn't the cover shot, Connor...because of the curse, you know. The cover curse."

"Bullshit, you'd give your left nut to be on the cover."

"Not me, you know what happened to Smokey LeBlanc after he was on the cover." Joe Dean tapped the framed cover of the baseball player, the shot that had split Stevie from Dex.

The Rev seemed puzzled. “I don’t remember anything happening to the Smoke.”

“He got married. And he was so young,” the quarterback replied in the same tone he would have used to mourn a friend who had gone to an early death.

The Rev rolled his big brown eyes. “Not likely to happen to you. No decent woman would have you. It’s time we had the celibacy talk.”

“Got to take a leak.” Joe Dean disappeared into Stevie’s bathroom and locked the door.

“You fellows have been so great. Can I offer you something to drink? I think I have Diet Coke, Bud Light, and maybe some milk, but that might have gone bad by now. You could go on down to the kitchen and I’ll catch up with you.” Stevie collected the dirty dishes from her coffee table.

Connor peered out the sitting room windows to the small yard filled with frost-browned banana trees and dead tropical plants. He stepped on to the tiny balcony accessed by a French door. The balcony overlooked two whiskey-barrel planters filled with ivy, rose-colored snapdragons, and yellow and purple pansies, the only flowers blooming at this season in a New Orleans winter. The flooring sagged a little under his weight. He looked over to an identical balcony in equally bad repair jutting out from Stevie’s bedroom and returned shaking his head.

“This is no good. You could get vertigo on those balconies and fall, or trip trying to get up and down the stairs. How are you going to put up groceries with all those steps to climb? Since I’m responsible for your condition, I think you should come home with me until you feel better. I have six bedrooms each with their own baths, two on the ground floor, and a great Jacuzzi on the deck that would be good for your bruises. My maid does all the cleaning and her mama cooks when I’m home. You could rest with me until you feel better.”

"Look, Connor, you're not responsible for what happened. I got in your way. Let's just go downstairs and see what there is to drink."

Connor Riley shrugged and started down the steps followed by Stevie and her dishes. The toilet flushed, even though Joe Dean had probably done nothing more than hide in the bathroom. When he came out, all Stevie's flowers were arranged precariously on the top of the commode. The Rev turned to look at the display and knocked against Stevie with one of his outsized elbows. She went tripping into Connor who caught her neatly in both arms. Her coffee mug crashed and broke to pieces at the bottom of the staircase.

"This is just what I meant," said Connor. "Why don't you pack a bag and come see my place? I swear I'm not putting the moves on you. We're in heavy training now and will be on the road most weekends. I won't be around much. Eula Mae and Miss Essie would take good care of you."

Stevie had to admit her heart was pounding, either from the close escape or the fact that Connor hadn't released her and she was still pressed against his chest—his broad, hard, warm chest. Sort of made a girl want to put her head down, close her eyes, and listen to his heartbeat. She gave in. "I'll pack a bag.

Chapter Four

Connor remained as good as his word. After installing Stevie in the downstairs guestroom with the king-sized bed and pink marble bath next to his suite, he went back to his training sessions and rarely spent much time at home. If Stevie felt a tiny bit disappointed, she could deal with it.

Miss Essie, the wiry brown chef, did not cook for invalids. She cooked for football players. She heaped Stevie's plate with food at each meal—mammoth portions of spaghetti with large oven-baked meatballs, rich Alfredos full of sliced chicken breast, jambalayas with chunks of lean ham or small, pink shrimp. The salad bowl remained ever full and a container of fresh fruit medley stayed always available in the refrigerator.

Fresh vegetables reigned, whatever looked good to Miss Essie in the French Market when she made her weekly trip. Dinner without exception finished with a dessert—a smooth sweet potato pie topped with whipped cream, strawberry shortcake with huge out-of-season berries, bread pudding six inches high with a cascade of hard sauce sluicing off the sides. Eula Mae, the maid, sacked containers of leftovers to take home each night and still gargantuan amounts remained for Connor to snack on when he came home tired and aching.

Concerned that Stevie seemed to have little appetite since she ate about a quarter of what he did, Connor asked one night, "Don't you like chicken Alfredo?"

"The trouble is I love chicken Alfredo, and it

loves me so much it goes right to my hips and stays there. I sort of stick to a high protein diet and deny my love of carbs. I thought you'd be more of a steak and eggs man."

"I would be if I could be. Got to carbo-load before the games. Essie can make you something else."

"How ungrateful would that make me? I don't even have to do my own laundry here."

"Eula Mae says you pick up after yourself and aren't any trouble. Sorry I'm not around much to keep you company."

"That's not your job. Winning games is. I'm fine, just a little antsy. I usually run every day and won't be able to do that until these ribs heal."

"I run during the off-season. Maybe we could train together some of the time."

Stevie laughed and brushed him off. "Like I could keep up with Connor Riley."

****

Intimate moments were few outside of meal times with the exception of sharing the Jacuzzi on a couple of occasions. Because Connor mentioned the Jacuzzi while trying to tempt Stevie to stay with him, she'd thrown an old tank suit into her suitcase along with any clean clothes she could find. She hated that suit, but the high neckline covered most of her bruises. So what if its lack of support allowed her breasts to plumb down and showed every bump in her nipples. She used the whirlpool for therapeutic reasons, not seduction.

Stevie kept a towel handy to wrap around her waist when she stepped out of the water. The electric blue fabric tended to stick in her crack, outlining each butt cheek perfectly. Connor did not seem to notice. He said little, just closed his eyes and leaned against the edge of the tub. Sometimes, he dozed off. So much for her sex appeal. She learned he had a light snore and slept like the dead without spending a single night with the man—more knowledge than many women who had casual sex knew about their partners.

On several evenings before the next big game, Joe Dean Billodeaux came over to watch and rewatch endless recordings of Dallas Cowboys' games on the big hi-def TV dominating one wall in the recreation room. The time to play billiards or foosball, pinball or video games came after the season playoffs ended. They invited Stevie to sit with them. Stifling her boredom as they tore the games apart minute by minute, she still enjoyed the company of two gorgeous men, especially when they ragged on each other.

The quarterback crowed when the next issue of *Sports Illustrated* arrived. "We got 'em nailed now. There's Shay Peyton on the cover, the Cowboys' quarterback in all his pretty boy glory. They've been cursed for sure."

Joe Dean could not contain his glee. He whooped several times and pounded Connor on the back.

"I thought I was the one who was cursed," Riley reminded him.

"This wipes out your curse, I think."

"I cannot believe even a Cajun could be this superstitious." Connor shook his head sadly.

"And you aren't? So how come you never get a real haircut during the season, just get your girly split ends trimmed, huh? And the Rev who trusts in the Lord so much he never takes off that cross his daddy blessed for him. If that's not superstition, I don't know what is. What do you say, Stevie?"

Stevie tended to sit quietly reading while they hashed over games and strategies and she refused to enter this debate. "To be honest, I think everyone has some small thing they hope will bring them luck. As for the cover curse, as a photographer I repudiate it utterly."

"She repudiates it utterly. What you t'ink dat means, *mon ami*?" Joe Dean scratched his head and did his dumb Cajun routine.

"It means she thinks you are a stupid, superstitious coonass who doesn't have a chance with her," Connor interpreted happily for him. Joe could be very appealing to women when he played dumb.

Stevie laughed at them both, gave each a sisterly peck on the cheek and a shoulder hug, and wished them a victory before she headed off to bed. They would be traveling to Dallas tomorrow and she would be watching the game on the enormous TV alone.

****

The game was an upset, a blowout, a tremendous victory for the supercharged Sinners. Connor carried the ball for three of the four touchdowns scored by his team, the other being made on an interception by defensive player Jerrol Whitney who scooped the ball out of the air and ran for it. The Cowboys managed only one touchdown and two field goals. In the after game interviews, Joe Dean shouted AAAA-EEEE into the mike and punched the air in his elation.

"This one's for Artie. I know you're watching, Art. I couldn't have beat them if you had still been on their team."

A female sportscaster shoved the mike in Connor's face. She asked who his game was for. Connor Riley looked directly into the camera. The close-up was so sharp Stevie could see his summer sky blue eyes and his blond curls dark with sweat.

"This one's for Stephanie," he said and quickly stepped back behind Coach Marty Buck so that man had to field the next question.

All over America, women wanted to be Connor Riley's Stephanie, she was sure. Sitting in his rec room, Stevie wished he hadn't called her Stephanie. Even so, her heart gave a small flutter in her bruised chest.

Chapter Five

The *Sports Illustrated* feature editor rarely missed a good story. Always being urged to increase readership with his selections, he knew Connor Riley was a guaranteed way to sell a few million newsstand copies to female readers who would never buy a subscription for themselves because they were offended by the swimsuit issue. He dispatched his most aggressive and fearless female reporter to request an interview with Riley at his luxurious home on Lake Ponchartrain outside of New Orleans. Rita Fortunado always got her story. This time would be no exception.

The reporter caught Joe Dean Billodeaux leaving as she arrived for the interview. Stevie, who had gone to the door with him, ducked back and peered out the sidelight. Joe Dean went right up to the reporter and demanded, "What has Riley got that I don't?"

Rita scraped a long, red varnished fingernail lightly down his cheek and promised, "Maybe I'll do you later."

"Maybe you will." Joe Dean bit her fingertip lightly and went away happy.

Stevie raced to the guestroom to hide out. She had a slight acquaintance with the reporter and had no intention of becoming part of her story. Still, if a girl needed fresh air on this mild January day when the air conditioners weren't running, the logical solution was to crack open a window. Not her idea to conduct the interview on the deck right outside of her bedroom.

Rita made herself at home on the cypress bench, asked Connor's permission to record the conversation, dated and identified the subject of the tape. She began by giving Riley a white, toothy smile outlined in man-eating red lipstick. She fluffed her thick, black hair with her long nails and started the interview.

"There is no doubt that you are having the best season of your professional career after being a first draft pick right out of LSU by the Sinners five years ago. To what would you attribute your success?"

"Um, a great coach, hard work,keeping my mind on the game, maturity."

"What about the rest of the Sinners?"

"We all do our part. We have a really strong defensive line this year, and Joe Dean Billodeaux and I work well together."

"I hear you are the only one of the Sinners' receivers who can catch his wild throws."

"Not all of them are wild. Joe has a strong arm and he's getting more control with experience. This is the first opportunity he's really had to show his stuff. We were sorry to lose Art Golden, though. This could have been Art's Super Bowl year."

"All of the above are undoubtedly true, but I have heard rumors that Connor Riley has a secret formula for success."

"Oh, I don't know about that."

"I've heard you have remained celibate this entire season. No groupies for Connor Riley. Is this true?"

Through the sheer curtains fluttering at her window, Stevie saw Connor color up as if he had just run ninety yards for a touchdown. Her own mind echoed Rita's question. Could this be true?

"Well, ah, yeah, it's true, but just this season." Connor seemed anxious not to appear to be some kind of freak.

"So, is this a religious thing or something else?

You are known on occasion to attend the church where Revelation Bullock's father preaches. Have you found Jesus?"

"No, it's not a religious thing, but it was the Rev's idea. He's had a great season, too, and is going to the Pro Bowl. Maybe you should ask him about this."

"But we are here now. So tell me, what does celibacy have to do with great football?"

"Okay, the Rev says it's a warrior thing. If you abstain from sex, all your aggression, all your concentration can be focused on winning. He says lots of societies have required their warriors to abstain from sex. In the Middle Ages, knights seeking the Holy Grail had to be pure, only in this case it's the Super Bowl we're seeking. Sounds weird when I say it out loud, but it works."

"The Sinners have quite a reputation for carousing in the French Quarter. Are any of your teammates also practicing celibacy? Say Joe Dean Billodeaux?"

"Not Joe, definitely not Joe, and none of the others that I've noticed. Some of the guys are married and don't fool around. I guess their wives wouldn't appreciate them taking a celibacy vow. It's only for the season though. Not afterwards, and the season is almost over, about five more weeks if we go all the way."

Connor noticed the open window and turned his back to it as if to hide Stevie from Rita Fortunado.

"You dedicated your last game to someone named Stephanie. Who might Stephanie be?"

"An old friend who was sick in the hospital for awhile, that's all. Could we talk about football?"

Rita had sunk her teeth in the subject and was not about to let go. "Just a guess, but are we talking about the photographer who goes by the name of Stevie Dowd, the woman you tackled a few weeks ago in the last of the regular season games? Stevie is an old friend of mine, too."

"No kidding?"

"Yes, I've been trying to reach her for days, but she isn't at her studio."

"She's, ah…maybe, she's recovering with family or friends. She was injured in the fall, concussion, cracked ribs, you know. And I didn't tackle her. I just sort of ran into her and fell on top of her with the Rev wrapped around my knees. Your magazine had a small article on it."

In the bedroom, Stevie breathed out quietly. Nice save, Connor, she thought. No way were she and Rita old friends. Mainly, they were two women trying to make it in a man's world, and Rita was doing better than her. She did not particularly like Rita, who sometimes traded sex for scoops.

"If you should see Stevie, tell her I hope she gets well soon." Rita looked pointedly over Connor's shoulder. Stevie stepped away from the window.

"Tell me, Connor, why are you still with the Sinners when you could have gone out as a free agent a couple of years ago? You've been playing good ball on a formerly losing team."

"Good ball, not great ball. This year I'm playing closer to my full potential, I think for the first time. Maybe a salary re-negotiation is in the future, but I grew up on this lake. I'd like to stay here and help the Sinners to another winning season. I want our victories to be part of the rebirth of New Orleans from the storm."

"Very noble of you with your yardage going up each week and your phenomenal number of touchdowns this season."

Relieved they'd returned to the subject of the game, Connor Riley sat back and appeared to enjoy the rest of the interview.

****

Naturally, Joe Dean brought the bad news. He arrived clutching the latest *Sports Illustrated,* flashing its cover at Stevie and rejoicing that the star receiver on the next team the Sinners were to meet graced the cover.

"Cursed, Kamal Mohammed is definitely cursed."

He tossed the magazine to Stevie who glanced at the teasers for the other feature articles. One of the bars read, *A Saint Among the Sinners?* She flipped through the contents. "Oh, no!"

There it was, Dexter Sykes' photo of her sprawled out on the ground with Connor Riley kneeling beside her like a knight in black armor. The layout was a full page bleed that made the legs of the medics and spectators fuzzy and vague like trees on a misty island. The picture had not been cropped and her nipples poked up visibly under her damp white T-shirt. To Connor's credit, his eyes appeared to be gazing raptly at her face. With her lips parted and her eyes half open, Stevie thought she looked as if she were recovering from a particularly good orgasm.

Joe Dean looked over her shoulder, his breath warm on her neck. "Hot shot, Stevie," he whispered in her ear. He raised his voice to get Connor's attention. "But Riley looks like a love-starved sap. Or maybe that should be sex-starved."

Connor crossed the room to take a look. "I'm sorry, Stevie. I know this must embarrass you."

"The camera does not lie. It's the article that worries me for your sake, not mine."

Connor leaned over Stevie and skimmed the article with her. It started out well enough with a short history of his career with the Sinners and his phenomenal season with new personal and team records set. Then came the celibacy issue, making that seem like the sole reason for his success, not hard work or experience.

Rita pointed out Connor did little drinking and was known for going home alone to his place on Lake

Pontchartrain after victory celebrations with the team. She pumped up his work with Habitat for Humanity and his visits to the children's ward while visiting Stevie. The reporter ended by saying a good source had told her Connor insisted on giving the female photographer he had injured a place to convalesce at his home.

According to Rita, Connor Riley lived alongside that woman like a pure warrior-knight, true to his vows. The woman's name was Stevie, short for Stephanie, Dowd, the woman to whom he had dedicated his last game. Yes, Connor Riley, truly a saint among the Sinners.

Joe Dean continued reading over Stevie's other shoulder. "Kind of makes you want to gag, huh? There will be letters to the editor next week about printing this chick stuff in a sports magazine, I guarantee you, me."

Stevie's cell phone rang. The gadget had remained fairly silent with the exception of a call or two from concerned friends once she cancelled her assignments for the next six weeks. She had not told anyone where she was recovering except her sister Michelle who had been sworn to secrecy. Stevie handed the magazine to Connor and moved a few feet away to take the call.

"Oh, hi, Mom. Well, I asked Michelle not to tell you I was injured. I didn't want you to worry… I'm sorry you had to find out about it in a national magazine. I didn't know you read *Sports Illustrated.* Thank my dear brother-in-law for showing you the picture… No, no, don't get on the bus. I'm well taken care of, feeling fine. I'm not shacked up, Mom. I'm recuperating… Yes, he is a nice boy, much nicer than Dex. No, you can't talk to him. He's not here. I swear I'll keep you up to date on my life from now on… Love you too, Mom. Bye."

Joe Dean's background snickers turned into a huge laugh. Pitching his voice high, he mocked,

"Connor Riley is such a nice boy. A saint among the Sinners."

"I don't suppose it was you who gave Rita her information about Stevie?" Connor asked, showing remarkable restraint.

Joe Dean looked down shamefaced. "She already knew or guessed. She came on to me real strong, and you know I'm not one to turn down a good offer. Hey, I'm the guy who said you weren't sleeping together. Don't I get some credit?"

"Let's go over the game tapes and forget it. Stevie, I'm sorry about this dick-head talking to Rita about you."

"Not your fault. I think I'll take a soak in the tub. You guys study your tapes. Big game coming up."

Stevie left the room and Connor tried to get back to business. He cued up a tape of their next opponents' last game, the one that moved them up in playoffs to meet the Sinners.

"Strong defense, hard hitters, fast runners. I think you should consider going to the short pass just over their line."

Joe Dean wasn't listening. Stevie, heading for the Jacuzzi, had walked past them out to the deck in her electric blue tank suit.

"Great legs, nice rack," he said appraisingly. "You can tell the breasts are real because they look all soft and squeezable. Can't believe you sit in that tub with her and don't get a hard-on."

Connor buried his face in his hands. "The game, Joe Dean, think about the game."

Chapter Six

Stevie watched the brutal game against the Salt Lake Saints. Joe Dean Billodeaux tried to stay with his favorite long passes to Connor Riley, but when the opposing team put three men on Riley, he created fumbles, over-throws, one interception, and many teeth-jarring tackles of the wide receiver. At the half, the score stood at seventeen-zip in favor of the Saints.

In the second half, Billodeaux saved his own ass with a fake and a run through a hole, gaining enough yardage to make a short pass into the end zone a possibility. Going to underutilized receiver, DeVon Deets, the Sinners got their first goal. A fierce defense kept the Saints from scoring again, and their attempt at another field goal failed.

Riley, taking over for the normal punt receiver, ran the ball back to the Sinners forty-yard line thanks to some great blocking. However, when Billodeaux attempted a throw to Riley on the next play, he was sacked with nowhere to go as defenders swarmed around the wide receiver. A series of short passes to Deets eventually got the touchdown.

In the fourth quarter, the Sinners needed one more. Billodeaux faked to Deets but found Connor open. He scored.

Stevie jumped up in front of Connor's wide-screen TV. She pumped her fist. "Yes, he scores!" She remembered her sore ribs and sat down again. Recuperation was becoming tedious, and she supposed Connor wouldn't be home until sometime tomorrow. He certainly didn't have to call or answer to her. The announcers had made a big deal about the Saints playing the Sinners. With no place in Salt Lake for the kind of victory celebration the Sinners team enjoyed, Connor would probably stay with Joe Dean in the city and go out with the team when they got home.

The big house was a lonely place with only the incessant shrill of the phone and the click of the answering machine taking endless messages ever since the magazine article appeared. Despite the number of calls, the messages sounded all about the same. "Connor, this is Brandi. Give me a call when the season is over." "Connor, this is Autumn. We spent a night together a couple of years ago. Here I thought you didn't like me, but now I understand. Let me leave my number in case you've lost it." "Hi Connor, Keely Hyde here. We went out a couple of times in college. Got your number from your mother. I'm working in New Orleans now. Give me a call sometime."

Feeling restless and edgy, Stevie went out to jog around the perimeter of Connor's walled and gated property. Her healing ribs demanded she stop before she got half way to the gate. She walked the rest of the way to use up some energy and quell whatever urges built inside her.

When she got back to the house, the phone was still ringing, the answering machine collecting more phone numbers from old flames and a few women who admitted they had never met Connor but had ferreted his number from acquaintances. A particularly candid lady named Caresse confessed she'd slept with Joe Dean Billodeaux to find out how to get in touch with Connor, the kind of man she really wanted.

To get away from the messages that were driving her slowly and surely nuts, Stevie headed to the hot tub where she could enjoy the peace of the night and the stars in the sky. She turned the deck lights low, slipped into the warm water and drifted off.

After looking around the house, Connor found her in the Jacuzzi. Blonde tendrils escaping from a mussed topknot floated in the water around her pale neck like the hair of a mermaid. Her lips, full and pink, were slightly parted. He didn't wake her but, limping slightly, went inside and got his trunks on. The backwash when he slid into the tub slapped Stevie in the face. She floundered awake to see Connor grinning at her across the tub.

Stevie wiped the water from her eyes. "I thought you wouldn't be home 'til tomorrow night. I must be reaching prune status by now." She contemplated her wrinkled fingertips.

"You look fine. I asked Coach if I could fly out right after the game. I guess you saw I got roughed up. I wanted to get home and soak the bruises. Got a sprain will have to be taped for the rest of the season. Not much longer now."

"Can I bring you something to eat? You can stay in the tub," she offered.

"No, I'm good."

"You certainly must be. The phone has been ringing all day and all night. I think the messages are being erased and recorded over. A lot of eager women out there are waiting for the end of the season."

"Damn Rita Fortunado. Like the hazing I'm getting from the guys isn't enough. They tried to get Joe Dean to give me one of his current women. He's running with a redhead who has a forty-four inch chest and just for balance, a skinny Tyra Banks super model look-alike right now. Joe said he isn't sharing. Didn't want to destroy my mojo, he said. And the trash talk I got about my saintliness from the opposing team, I don't even want to repeat. Stevie, I'm not a saint."

"That's what all these women who are calling seem to know." She flicked a small spray of water at him, but the droplets only hit mid-chest and meandered down through his golden hair and back into the tub just above his waist. Stevie followed the trickle with her eyes.

"And I'm not your brother's college girl friend anymore. I've been around, Connor. The funny thing is I might have ended up married to Kevin if he had known I got a prescription for birth control pills that week. I was waiting for my next period so I could start them, Kevin's Christmas surprise. I got the surprise when he dumped me, so I took my pills and went to study in Italy.

"I didn't need to know that." Connor knew his face flushed. From the heat of the water, he told himself. Regardless, Stevie went full steam ahead. Stephanie Dowd, no shrinking violet.

"And then, there was Marcello who wanted to be a male model. I created a great portfolio for him, dressed and undressed. He did leave me a note of thanks for the good times and the great photos when he took off for New York. You know about Dexter Sykes. We were partners in the studio and in bed. He stole my Smokey LeBlanc cover. I don't think saintly men exist. I need to get out now. I really do."

Stevie heaved herself out of the water. The tank suit immediately plastered itself against her body and revealed her raised nipples, the small dent of her navel and the cleft between her legs. She bent to get her towel and gave Connor the rear view as well.

"Do you know why I always stay in the tub for awhile after you get out? Because I can't get out without embarrassing the both of us. I still covet my brother's college girlfriend."

Connor stood, his desire obvious. He reached up, grasped Stevie by the waist and pulled her back into the tub. He slid down into the water and held her along the length of his body, his aroused penis pressed against the cleft between her legs. He wrapped both of his muscular arms about her as if she might try to escape, and drove his lips against hers, his tongue seeking immediate entrance.

She had been celibate longer than Connor. She moved against him with her legs planted wide over his hips. They had to give up the kiss to suck in enough air to keep breathing. Connor loosened his arms and put his head back, eyes closed. He jerked when Stevie bit his shoulder, but pressed her harder against him with his hands on her buttocks.

He could not stop himself. It had been such a long time. He shuddered and cried, "Oh, God!"

But Stevie wasn't finished and she wasn't stopping. Connor tried to lift her, but she clung tightly to his hips, moving against him faster and faster. The slick fabric of the bathing suit sunk deep into her cleft seemed to add to her pleasure. And then it happened, that tight contraction, that the infinite expansion only women experienced,going on and on until she collapsed against his chest.

Connor took her in his arms and raised her to the lip of the tub. He buried his face in her lap. Stroking his long blond curls, Stevie let herself slip back against the cool planks of the deck. A few moments later, Connor heaved himself out of the water and lay on the deck beside her. They touched at shoulder, hip and fingertips. Both looked up at the stars.

"Did I hurt you? You know, your ribs. I sort of lost track of where my hands were going."

"I'm not feeling any pain. None at all. But look, I'm sorry if I made you break your vow. I wasn't trying to get first in line for the end of the season or anything like that. It's been a long time between lovers for me, too."

"Hell, President Clinton wouldn't even consider this to be sex. I keep telling people the celibacy thing wasn't a vow, but nobody hears me. I just hope those old stories about women getting pregnant in swimming pools aren't true. I wasn't exactly a model of control tonight."

"Chlorine will get those little buggers, I guess...I hope. I stopped taking the pill after I threw Dex out. No sense filling your body with chemicals when you've given up on men, right?"

"Uh, right. I have a whole box of condoms in my night table. We could go check the expiration date on them together."

"Sounds like a great plan to me."

The condoms had not expired. Stevie stretched out beside Connor and rested her head against his chest. He looked down the length of her naked body nestled against him and admired her full, pink-tipped breasts, the light unwaxed curls between her legs, those long, smooth limbs. Stevie Dowd, one-hundred percent natural woman and all his.

"Ah, Stevie. I'm kind of beat from the game and the travel time, and I'm no Superman. I might need a little time to recuperate, but if you want, I can take care of-um-your needs again."

"No Superman, but definitely a saint. I don't recall any man ever saying that to me before. If word gets out, that phone will start ringing again. They won't hear it from me. I want to keep you all to myself for awhile."

"That's the way I want it, too."

"Let's get some rest. Maybe later tonight." Stevie snuggled even closer and simply fell asleep.

Connor stroked her long, blonde hair still damp from the tub and tangled from their last encounter. He'd given her something Kevin never had. Now this tough, independent woman belonged to him, not his brother. She would not appreciate being treated like some fragile female. He was no expert on women like Joe Dean, but he did know that. Still, what he felt for her was a deep tenderness and the desire to protect, something pretty close to love. But then, he'd been searching for Stevie Dowd all of his adult years while she went unaware with other men who had hurt her. Time, he had to give her some time whether he wanted to or not. Keeping her near, he closed his eyes.

Stevie woke around three in the morning. Pressed up against her, Connor snored lightly. She should return to her own bed and let him rest. Carefully, she raised the heavy arm that enclosed her and slipped to the edge of the mattress. Connor rolled on to his back. The shine from the security lights outside the house pierced through the windows and gilded his tall, pale body. Even flaccid he was an exciting man to behold. Ah, those bold Viking cheekbones, those sculpted lips, the light stubble beginning to appear on his chin that would give a slight scratch to any lovemaking. Not to mention what he had between his legs. Nothing to complain about there. No, indeed.

She wanted to lean over and kiss his lips, wake him for more bed sports, but she also noticed his bruises, that taped ankle. She must let him recuperate. She could always finish up alone just by remembering him. Connor Riley, a man who would be too easy to love. She shifted her weight and stood up.

His eyes opened. His hormones kicked in. Looking at her naked body with drowsy eyes, he said, "I think we should use those condoms before they go bad."

"You should rest."

"I don't need rest as much as I need you."

"Fine, I'm easy to convince and ready just looking at you."

Stevie spread herself out on the bed again and Connor, fresh condom applied, rolled atop. He started slowly making sure of that readiness, careful of her sore ribs.

Oh yes, so much better without the bathing suit and swimming trunks between them, Stevie thought. Better than Dex or Marcello. And who cared about Kevin Riley anymore?

Chapter Seven

Obviously, Joe Dean Billodeaux was not the happy team player this evening. He slumped in a lounge chair on Connor's deck and glumly watched Riley flip steaks on the grill where three thick porterhouses and one rib eye sizzled. Connor knew he wore a cheese-eating grin and gave himself away every time he looked at Stevie. Frankly, he didn't give a damn what kind of foul mood Joe was in, nothing could take the shine from having Stevie in his bed last night.

The quarterback regaled everyone on the deck with his complaints. "Sure, after the game review, the rest of you guys did a light workout and went home. Coach Buck says, 'Oh, Connor stay off your bad ankle', but I get held back. I spent all afternoon throwing pass after pass to DeVon Deets, long ones, short ones, left field, right field. Next practice, Coach wants me to concentrate on handing off to the halfback as if I'm some new kid in high school. 'Pretend there is no Connor Riley on the team', Coach says. My performance isn't our big problem. You know what our problem really is?"

"What?" the Rev asked. He'd driven in from his mama's house in Chapelle for the cookout. Not being in training, and being far from his father's church, the big man sucked on his third beer.

Joe Dean still nursed his first drink. "Sure, I'm tired today after that hard game and that little victory celebration. Amber went home early. She had a six a.m. modeling call. Misty stayed until four when I asked her to go home so I could get some sleep. Tired isn't the problem, no."

The Rev rolled his big, brown eyes and asked again, "What is the problem, Joe?"

"Say Con, where's the grim warrior face I've been seeing at all season?" Joe chafed. "Where did it go?"

"Just happy I didn't have to work out with you all afternoon, Joe."

"Our problem is you nailed Stevie last night, didn't you? Now all your mojo is gone. That's our problem. If I'd known you were going to give in this late in the season, I'd have let you have Misty. The boobs aren't real, but they're still nice to look at." Joe glanced around cautiously to see if Stevie had come back from checking on her place in the city.

"Misty's chest is bigger around than mine. Those boobs had to be fake. And I did not nail Stevie." Connor held the meat fork up like a weapon ready to use.

"Well, if not nail, then screw or fuck her?" Joe Dean persisted.

The Rev frowned. Connor's grim warrior face returned. "It's none of your damn business. I don't ask what you do with your bimbos."

The Rev got up and casually took the meat fork from Connor's hand. "Let the expert grill."

"Oh, no! Do not tell me you *made love* with Stevie." Joe Dean drilled a dimple in his chin with his little finger and fluttered his eyelashes. "This is bad, really bad. You fall off the celibacy bandwagon with two games left to play, and it's not just good old theraputic sex, it's looove. How are you gonna keep your mind on the game, tell me that?"

"Joe, let Connor be. He wouldn't break his oath." The Rev startled when Connor turned on him.

"Yeah, it's easy for you, Rev. Your season's been over for a month. You're probably getting plenty back in old Chapelle. And it wasn't an oath! Celibacy was a strategy to improve my game. I would keep an oath."

"As a matter of fact, I haven't been with anybody and I'll tell you why." The Rev took advantage of their stunned expressions. "I've met the woman I am going to marry."

"And you haven't tried her out yet?" Joe Dean said with amazement.

"There I was sitting in my mama's kitchen watching her fry up the Sunday chicken. Granny was on her way over with a big yellow bowl of my favorite cornbread dressing. A big mess of greens full of bacon cooked on the back burner and my Aunt Lizzie's cold banana pudding chilled in the fridge. I was a happy man until my mama says we are having a special guest over for dinner. That always means she's trying to fix me up with someone and get herself some grandkids. Suddenly, Burger King for lunch looked mighty good."

"Those steaks about ready? You're making me hungry," Joe Dean asked.

"All in good time," said the Rev. "Eat some peanuts. As I was saying, I thought about heading out when Mama tells me the guest is the new community doctor, one of these med students who gets a free ride, then has to work in a rural area for some years to pay it back. Okay, it's a man, I think, and relax. Then, in walks Arminta Green, Dr. Green."

"And she was dazzled to meet a famous football player living right there in Chapelle, Louisiana," Connor said.

"Nope. She doesn't follow the game. Been studying and doctoring for years with no time to watch TV. Didn't recognize my name even when Mama dragged her into the living room to show her my albums. I had to finish frying the chicken."

His audience laughed. They looked at the opening door to the deck and saw Stevie about to rejoin the group. The Rev cranked up his narrative a notch.

"So there I am sitting across from this light-skinned lovely with green eyes and soft, beautiful light brown hair that didn't even look like it had been straightened. I could hardly finish my fourth piece of chicken for staring at her. We get to the cold banana pudding and I say, 'Miss Min-tay, would you like to take a drive in the country in my Cadillac Escalade, see some of the town?' She says no. Got an early clinic in the morning and wants to get some rest. 'Maybe some other time.'"

"How many times have you taken her out since then?" Stevie asked sliding on to a bench next to Connor. Riley automatically put an arm around her shoulders. Joe Dean glared.

"None, not once. Dr. Green does not impress easily, but I think I'm making some headway. I been driving the elderly who have no transportation over to her clinic. Then, I have to wait around to take them back. I get in a few words. She can't help but notice what a good guy I am. I mean, some of them old folks is real nasty. I think one of them peed on my car seat. But, I'm gonna make my mama proud. I plan to marry a doctor."

Stevie laughed. Joe Dean took a turn rolling his eyes. Connor smiled and tightened his hold on Stevie's shoulders.

"How do you know this is love and not just plain horniness?" Joe Dean queried.

"Because I can get rid of my lust anytime with anyone, but I only want to do it with Dr. Arminta Green. Connor knows what I mean."

The noise of a speedboat coming towards Connor's dock drowned out any comment. Driven by a young woman who appeared to be topless—no, definitely was topless, the boat veered close. Two more women, judging by age, college students on semester break stood up holding a banner made from a bed sheet. The lettering read, "Call us first,

Connor" and listed their phone numbers. They dropped the sheet directly across from the men to show their naked bodies. While not particularly well endowed, they were young, slender and nubile. One was a real redhead unless she used dye in unusual places.

Joe Dean scribbled the phone numbers on a paper napkin before he could forget them. Connor stared straight ahead, watching his sailboat and ski boat bob in the wake. The Rev shook his head in disgust as he watched the young women pulling on bikini bottoms and T-shirts, their giggles coming across the water on the wind.

"I'm sorry you had to see that, Stevie." Connor took her hands in his.

"I'm twenty-nine. I can't compete with that," she said, joking, sort of.

"Yes, you can. You more than do," Connor assured her, gazing into Stevie's eyes.

"That leaves all three for me, then. I can handle that," Joe Dean claimed, but he still fretted. "Connor, you just keep your focus on the game and don't slip up again. That cover curse could still be in effect, you see, a double whammy because you broke that vow. Might be too, too much for one Cajun boy to fix."

"It wasn't a vow! No worries, Joe Dean, no worries." Connor planted a kiss on Stevie's cheek.

A cool breeze wafted off the lake. Stevie shivered and Connor snugged her against his side.

To lighten the mood, she said, "It's a wonder those girls weren't blue and goose-bumped. Then, I could compete."

But what if Stevie Dowd had cost the Sinners the Super Bowl last night?

Chapter Eight

Coach Buck paced in front of his team. He stopped and faced them giving Connor and Joe Dean the eye. “This is the big one that could take us to the Super Bowl, boys. Now, y’all know I’ve been working Joe hard, making him try new moves, and letting Riley get some rest. It don’t matter what they do if all of you ain’t at your best, too. For my part, I think we got the best defense in the league and more fine receivers than the Packers expect. But, it’s their home field, Lambeau Field, one of the truly great stadiums. It’s twenty degrees out there with snow on the ground, something us southern boys ain’t used to. Their fans will cheer you deaf. So, I’m saying, tune out the crowd. Forget the snow. Keep your mind on the game, and go out there and win!”

****

Back at the Lake Ponchartrain house, Stevie Dowd again watched the game on Connor’s big screen TV. This was the kind of playoff game fans relished, hard fighting for yardage punctuated with dramatic breakouts and passes. Few passes came to Connor Riley. Billodeaux listened to his coaches. He faked when they wanted a fake, passed off the ball for a charge through the line when told to, and threw his passes to DeVon Deets who eventually scored the two touchdowns that had the Sinners one up on Green Bay going into the second half.

Stevie enjoyed the game, screaming herself hoarse in the large, empty house. The phone didn’t bother her. Presumably, all of Connor’s old girlfriends were glued to the TV just as she was.

She wondered if they had the urge to touch the screen every time the cameras panned to a bench shot showing Connor huddled under a parka, his blond hair falling forward across his cheeks from under the edge of the black hood. He never took his eyes from the field. Stevie wanted to reach up and bush his hair back with her fingertips, then warm his hands and tell him she waited for him back in New Orleans where it was fifty degrees outside and much warmer inside. Thinking that way put her on the road to more heartbreak. She needed to move back to her studio and quickly before she became just one more of his off-season women.

The second half started. Obviously, the cold and the hard play had taken its toll on the Sinners. Green Bay scored twice in the third quarter. During the break, they had rethought their defense and adjusted to the Sinners' new tactics. The defense gave Deets no room to run. Billodeaux was sacked twice.

The Sinners' defense pulled itself together and kept the Packers from scoring for most of the fourth quarter. They saw to it their offense would have one last chance at a goal in the last minutes of the game. Then it happened. The long, long pass Joe Dean had been saving up rocketed into the arms of the lightly guarded and supposedly injured Connor Riley who stood right there waiting for it. Riley streaked into the end zone and spiked the ball. Ancient Andy kicked the extra point and the game went into overtime.

Once again, the Sinners' defense dug in and held the line until the ball turned over to their team again. Their offense struggled down the field with both Deets and Riley well-covered. In the end, the golden toe of Andy Mortenson kicked a ball rock hard with the cold between the posts to send the Sinners on to the Super Bowl.

"Amazing, from wild card team to Super Bowl.

Coach Buck can you explain how this happened?" the sportscaster asked, shoving his mike into Buck's face. Coach Buck, an old hand with reporters, took control and seized the mike.

"Quarterback Art Golden saw us through our infant years as an expansion team. He gave us a decent season this year, too, but young Joe Dean Billodeaux—now that's a tongue-twister of a name, I call him Joe most times—gave the Sinners the extra spark that got us here. Young don't necessarily mean better, Cal." Coach waved the mike toward the team's owner. "You need your coach well-seasoned and your kickers well-aged. Couldn't have done it without Andy Mortenson. Deets and Riley played their best game. There are no finer receivers in the league."

Green Bay's fans gave their team a standing ovation. Over the roar, the reporter hauled Connor from the crush and pressed the mike on him. "Most of us assumed you were playing hurt after last week's rough and tumble game, Connor. We all thought we detected a slight limp when you came on the field. Would acting be another one of your talents?"

"I took some hard hits last week, have a taped ankle. But right now, I'm feeling no pain, none at all." Connor stared right into the camera as if he were making eye contact with Stevie—and half a million other women.

"Would you like to dedicate this game to anyone, Connor?" the sportscaster asked slyly.

"Sure would. This one's for you, Mom."

The newsman laughed and headed off to push his way through the throng surrounding Joe Dean Billodeaux.

"Joe Dean, great game, but not your usual game. What's going on?"

"Well, I practiced hard on some new plays and listened to my coaches. I was glad I could do what they asked of me. And Stevie, no hard feelings, sugar." Joe Dean aped a big smacking kiss.

Across America, Stevie was sure women who watched football alone pressed their lips to the screen. She sighed and shook her head as Joe Dean's face gave way to DeVon Deets' visage. She should pack right now and go back to her place even if it meant borrowing one of Connor's vehicles. The keys were all kept on the pegboard for the fully-loaded black luxury SUV with the custom red pin-striping, the low-slung Jaguar with the same custom paint, and the 4x4 truck with the winking red devil on the tailgate. No, he had driven that one to the airport. The red Honda motorcycle didn't have enough room for her suitcase. Yes, she definitely must leave before she got used to living like this with the guy who was too easy to love.

****

When Connor arrived home the next afternoon, Stevie was still there. She would have been ungrateful to leave without saying good-bye she'd rationalized all night long. Stevie asked Miss Essie to prepare a special meal involving the sacrifice of two heavy-tailed lobsters into a pot of boiling water, a tray of roasted oysters, slim bundles of asparagus, hot French bread, and a vat of chocolate mousse. Champagne for a beverage was a given. This might as well be a night to remember.

Connor parked in the drive and charged up the three wide flagstone steps fronting his house, no sign of a limp in his gait now. Stevie stood just inside the door. He lifted her by the waist, swung her around once, then carefully set her down again. He held up a thermos. "Brought you something."

Stevie uncapped the jug. "What is it?"

"Snow from Lambeau Field!" Connor upended the contents into his big hand. He squeezed the frozen mass into a small ball and shoved it between Stevie's breasts showing some cleavage above her little knit top.

"Brute!" She poured the rest of the slush on his head and took off running.

Connor tossed the thermos to a wide-eyed Eula Mae and trotted off after Stevie giving her enough time to reach the bedroom, but not enough to get the door locked. There followed a great deal of laughing and the sound of bed springs being punished.

By the time the couple exited the bedroom, Eula Mae, twice the size of her tiny Mama Essie and a great deal darker, had mopped up the slush.

"Sorry," Stevie apologized sheepishly to the maid who waited to serve dinner.

"Ain't as if I never seen anything like that before, but the past year been mighty quiet, Miss Stevie. That man is ripe for the picking. Well, looks like those lobsters Mama has on ice have lost their last reprieve. I'll go tell her you ready to eat now."

Stevie nodded. Of course that's all she was, a handy form of relief for Connor after a long dry spell. Good thing she intended to leave in the morning.

****

Connor sent Eula Mae and her mama home long before they got to the dessert. What remained of the beautiful presentation of chocolate mousse piped with whipped cream and served in a crystal bowl sat between them on the bed. Connor fed her dollops of the pudding scraped from the sides of the bowl and served on his fingertips. The rest of the rich dessert smeared the sheets.

Connor had started the food fantasy just as he had the snowball fight. First, he suggested they take dessert into the bedroom, then that they eat it in the nude—and then, that they eat it off each other. He coated her fair skin, the bruises all gone by now, with the chocolate from breast to bottom. She slathered him from chest to groin. They licked the chocolate pudding off until they could not stand their growing sensitivity and had to move on to the main course—each other.

The pudding made for an interesting lubricant and a sticky aftermath. Ever mindful of her injured ribs, Connor placed Stevie over him. He dangled the remaining stemmed cherry in front of her mouth. She inhaled it, leaving the stem between her lips as she rolled the fruit on her tongue. Connor's prick gave an appreciative flip.

"He should be exhausted." Stevie ran a finger down Connor's centerline through hair matted with chocolate. She got another flip. The mousse streaked her hair and his, the sheets soggy with all manner of fluids. Clearly, having a well-paid maid was worth the money. If Stevie had been at her place, she would have worried all night about getting the stains out of the linens and cleaning up the mess, shades of her mother interfering with her pleasure. She sighed. She was going to miss this, and Connor, lovely Connor, most of all.

"If nothing else proves it, this does. I am well and I cannot keep sponging off of you this way."

"Sponging off. Good idea. Let's hit the shower, then move to your bedroom," Connor answered not really following her drift. He twined her hair around his fingers and sucked the chocolate from the tips.

"I mean I should return to my own place. I need to get back to work before I have no work to go back to. Are you listening?" She raised his heavy head between her hands.

Connor took that as an invitation for a long, deep kiss. Despite his bumps, bruises and taped ankle, his body said ready to go again. Careful not to put his full weight on her, he went on top this time. He moved over her, nudging her legs apart with his knees, and thrust. Keeping himself suspended above her, he pumped. He worked his thighs and hips and bore his weight with his biceps.

"This could become a very popular training exercise. Hell, Billodeaux probably already uses it to strengthen his arms," he joked, making her laugh.

Stevie gave in and closed her eyes. She ran her hands over his straining biceps and enjoyed his strength. When her climax began to build, she dug her fingernails into his upper arms and hung on until the spasms passed. They could talk tomorrow.

****

Connor left before Stevie managed to get out of bed and give her hair another washing. His attempt to clean her up last night had only led to shower sex. He'd never make a good shampoo guy. The ones she knew were all gay. Glancing into his room as she straggled towards the kitchen, she noticed fresh sheets on his bed and a clean new spread turned back and inviting. Did he have a closet full of them for these occasions? The crystal bowl had long joined others dishes in the washer. Miss Essie greeted Stevie at the breakfast table as if nothing odd had occurred. Maybe mousse-encrusted beds were the norm in Connor Riley's household. She must remember that and pack her bags.

By the time Connor returned full of good humor, she had actually started to get her things together. He loomed in the door of the guestroom, eyeing her suitcase open on the bed.

"Great, you can travel with my family to the Super Bowl, but you don't have to pack right now. We have some training this week, then fly out to Seattle the week before the game. Got to get used to the FieldTurf at Seahawk Stadium. My folks rented one of those floating houses they have out there. It has four bedrooms and I don't think Merrilee is taking the two younger kids. Let me give Mom a call. I know she'll squeeze you in."

"I could not possibly stay with your mother and Kevin's family. I really need to get back to work before I can't make my rent."

"So, you can cover the Super Bowl and won't have to pay for a hotel room. I'll see you get a press pass. Don't miss out on a great deal." He strode across the room, shoved the suitcase and its contents to the floor and pulled Stevie into his arms.

"Oh, Connor, what am I going to do with you?" Stevie rested her head on his broad chest.

"If you are out of ideas, I have some suggestions," he answered.

Chapter Nine

Because of crowded flights into Seattle, Stevie took the red-eye leaving at 5:00 a.m. the day before the Super Bowl. She couldn't get on the same flight as Ma and Pa Riley, traveling with Brother Kevin, Merrilee and an eight-year-old nephew and six-year-old niece. If she were honest, she hadn't tried very hard to do so. This whole arrangement would be awkward enough.

When the cab pulled up near the designated address, Stevie reluctantly gathered her gear and started down the boardwalk. The house number matched the one on a cheerful yellow two-story floating home at the very end of the pier. She rang the bell on the green door set between two planters of yellow and purple pansies blooming abundantly in the chill air. The door swung open and she stepped into the two welcoming arms belonging to Connor's mother and the chaos beyond her.

"Stephanie Dowd, we meet at last," the tall blonde woman said in greeting. Her voice had a slight accent hinting of Sweden, but Connor claimed was really northern Wisconsin in origin. "I'm Kristen Riley, Connor's mom."

Kristen Riley had aged like a loftier version of Grace Kelly. Once a Golden Girl for the old Saints team, she had put on flesh in her middle years but still had beauty and style. Her eyes were Connor's eyes, the beautiful cerulean blue of a northern sky on a sunny winter's day. Her lips were Connor's, full and beautifully formed. Her nose, like his, set straight and slim. By now, she should have touches of gray in her hair, but she kept it tinted a tasteful champagne blonde. She wore its soft waves pulled back into a knot at the base of her neck. Her long legs remained shapely though her waist had thickened and her rather impressive breasts overflowed in grandmotherly abundance. She hugged Stevie to that pillowy chest.

Pulling slightly away, Stevie smiled at her welcome. "I'm happy to meet you, Mrs. Riley. Connor is so fond of you," she said over the background noise of a television and crying children.

"Sure, a man should love his mother and his wife. Connor has plenty of love to go around. You should see him with his nieces and nephews. Connor will make a great father someday, the sooner the better. Sorry we haven't met before, but I try to give my son his privacy. He is a young man and, well...young men need privacy. I wouldn't want to walk in on anything, you know. We talk on the phone nearly every day, and lately all the talk is of the wonderful Stephanie Dowd. Come in, come in."

Stevie stood as if glued to the doorstep. Mrs. Riley gave her arm a tug and ushered her into the living room where the rest of the family gathered: big, burly Keith Riley, Connor's dad, and petite, brunette Merrilee, the woman Kevin Riley married after dumping Stevie. Children swarmed around them. Stevie counted four on the floor, and looking at Merrilee from the bottom up, number five was due in about four months.

Beneath a pile of kids, Kevin Riley of the dark hair and Irish eyes gave horsey rides to two of his brood. The two-year old boy, who had his daddy's dark hair and deep blue eyes, had just fallen off and wailed loudly.

A little girl with dark curls and darker eyes attempted to pull her four-year-old sister off Daddy's back. "My turn, my turn!" she shrieked. An eight-year-old boy, also dark haired and dark-eyed, sat by his mother in a folded-arm pose. Obviously, he was too old for horsey rides, but a little jealous of the cuddling his baby brother got for falling.

Mrs. Riley clapped her hands for attention. “This is Stephanie Dowd, Connor’s special friend. I want you to make her feel like part of the family.”

“Stevie. Please, call me Stevie, all of you. I see you decided to bring all of the grandchildren and won’t have room for me. Let me see if the cab is still there. I can go to a hotel.” Their guest backed towards the door, but she was not allowed to escape.

“The every hotel in the city is booked for the game.” Keith Riley waded through the children, his hand held out to shake hers. “The kids can share a room, the girls in the bed, the boys on the floor. Merrilee decided to bring them all at the last minute. Let me tell you, it was a miserable trip. We had to take turns holding the youngest since the plane was full to capacity.” He frowned at his daughter-in-law while grasping Stevie’s hand and pumping it.

Merrilee rose, taking the two-year-old with her. She settled the child straddle-legged across her rounded belly and patted his back. Behind her, Kevin of the sparkling, clever blue eyes sat up, the four-year-old girl with the bouncing curls nestled in his lap. Merrilee stood in front of her husband blocking the view.

“So pleased to meet you, Stevie. This is Colby,” she said, introducing the shy little boy hiding his face on her shoulder. “And Katherine, my oldest daughter.” She pulled the six-year-old forward. “On the couch is Collin, our first-born. That’s Cameron in her daddy’s lap. And my husband, Kevin, of course.” Merrilee freed one hand to pat her belly. “This one is going to be Courtney.” She smiled as if she had never heard of a Stephanie Dowd who dated her husband for three months prior to their marriage.

Kevin rose, letting his younger daughter slip

down and cling to his leg. He towered over his wife. Another six-foot plus like his brother, Kev had filled out in the last nine years. By middle-age he would have his father's big build and probably his receding hairline, too. The great Irish blue eyes and sly, suggestive smile would never change. Once, Stevie had found that smile irresistible.

"Stephanie," he greeted. "It's great to see you again. I was always sorry about the way things went with us. I never really explained, that well…Collin was on the way, and I had to do my duty, as my father likes to say."

Merrilee turned and glared at him. Stevie waved her hand in the air as if she could erase his statement.

She stumbled over her words trying to ease the situation. "Bygones. Water under bridge. And, ah, I can see you are really good at fathering, at fatherhood, I mean. So many children would overwhelm me, but I can see you and Merrilee have it all under control."

The four-year-old left her father's leg and made her way through the forest of adults. She stopped directly in front of Stevie, put her arms on her small hips, and blurted out, "Mommy doesn't like you. Go away." Stevie backed up.

"Cammie, you are being very rude to Uncle Connor's friend. I know you like Uncle Connor and wouldn't want him to be mad at you. Say sorry to Stevie," Kristen Riley insisted.

"Sorry," the child repeated insincerely.

"Good girl. Now Stevie, let me show you to your room. Connor is going to stop by when he can, but he's staying with the team tonight. You must be very tired after getting up so early."

Stevie said she was. In fact, she thought she would take a long nap, a long, long nap until Connor arrived.

****

The sound of small feet racing up and down the hallway kept Stevie from sleeping. At some point in the endless afternoon, a light knock sounded on the bedroom door and Mrs. Riley's voice asked if she was awake. Stevie laid still and silent until Connor's mother left.

Around five, she tried again. "Stevie, dear, we're all going to some famous restaurant for fish and chips. You can't do fancy when you have small children along, but won't you join us?"

Stevie sat up, groggy from finally dozing. Running her fingers through her mussed hair, she went to the door to face Kristen Riley. "Thanks for the offer, but I'm really jet-lagged. If there's food in the kitchen, I'll make myself something later. I had one of those eight-dollar sandwiches on the plane for lunch so I'm not starving. Besides, Miss Essie fed me too well while I was recovering. I need to take off the five pounds cemented to my hips." Stevie chuckled to keep things friendly.

Kristen Riley sighed. "I remember when it was just five pounds I had to lose. Ah well, Keith says he loves all of me and always has from the first time he saw me. Did Connor ever tell you how his father and I met?"

"No." Stevie moved aside since the woman seemed determined to come into the room.

Mrs. Riley settled herself on the edge of the bed that sank a bit under her weight. Stevie took a chair from the small writing desk near the window. The least she could do was listen to the woman's reminiscence. She couldn't fault Kristen for this awkward situation Connor had created. The game was tomorrow. Stevie could visit some of Seattle, cover the Super Bowl, then take a cab to the airport and see if a space on a red-eye back to New Orleans had become available. She would go directly to her studio and stay there where she belonged.

"Well, I had just graduated from the University

of Wisconsin where I earned some of my expenses performing as a cheerleader. I wanted to travel and see some of the world, so I tried out to cheer for the Saints. I know, often not so much to cheer about. New Orleans is so hot and steamy, like a foreign country to a northern girl. The judges liked my long legs, and of course, my big breasts, but said I looked too corn-fed and needed to lose twenty pounds to make the squad. They took me on as an alternate. I worked hard and lost those twenty pounds, which is not so easy in New Orleans with all the good food, but I did. When one of the other girls sprained an ankle, I got to perform."

Stevie wondered how long this story would take as Mrs. Riley went on.

"I was picked up on the big screen for one of those honey shots, they call them. Keith sat up in a luxury box his engineering firm rented and saw me. He said to his boss, 'That's the woman I am going to marry,' just like that. He got my name and waited for me after the game."

Kristen Riley smiled fondly. "I had been in New Orleans a few months now and heard that line pretty often in the bars around town, even in the department store where I worked. You know, 'I want you to have my baby' and other nonsense from young men and some old ones, too. I tried to ignore him, but Keith persisted until he got my number. He courted me until football season ended, fairly soon for the Saints in those days. I knew from the first night we dated this was the man for me. We were engaged on New Year's Eve and married in June. Three months later, I was expecting Kevin, and two years later, Connor was on the way. It was that simple for us. Love at first sight for Keith and a soul mate for me."

"That's a lovely story, Mrs. Riley." Stevie smiled wistfully. "You must have been very beautiful. You still are."

"No more than you. I suppose being a modern career woman, you don't believe in love at first sight or soul mates really, do you?"

"I did once—when I was a silly college girl a long time ago."

"It would be my Kevin's fault you no longer believe such a thing is possible."

"And Marcello's and Dexter's, some other guys in my life. Let's not put all the blame on Kevin. The night I met Kevin, he said those same words to me. 'Marry me and have my babies.' I knew it was a line, but after a few hours with him, I wanted to believe him. Turned out I was only his rebound girl after his breakup with Merrilee the week before. He said she cheated on him, but now he had found someone better. We were over in three months and back he went to Merrilee. End of story."

"No, I don't think it was," Mrs. Riley disagreed. "At the age of seventeen, Connor told me all about you. I guess he was tattling on his brother, too, for having you over when he knew we were out of town, but there was more to it. Connor said he had met the woman he wanted to marry just the way his dad had, love at first sight. He was an athlete and very popular with young ladies of his own age. We laughed it off as a crush on an older woman. Then, of course, Kevin broke up with you before you could meet the whole family. Things moved very fast after that with Merrilee who had been a part of Kevin's life for two years. I guess she didn't want to take any chances on losing him again. We don't regret our grandson, naturally."

"Naturally. Kevin has beautiful children." Again, Stevie gazed wistfully at Kristen Riley.

"You would have thought Connor would forget about you, a girl he met only once, but he told me after he went to LSU that he looked for you. You weren't in the student directory. He asked Kevin for your address and phone number. Kevin claimed he had thrown it away. Later, he found Kevin's old address book, but new girls were living in your apartment. They didn't know where you had gone."

"Italy. I was studying in Italy. I barely came home to get my diploma, then went right back. Marcello waited for me."

"I think Connor tried to find you through the alumni association, too, but your home address was no longer any good."

"My father passed away a few months after I returned from Italy. Heart attack. He was a big sports fan. He would have loved to see the work I'm doing now. Mom moved to Houston to be near my married sister and her grandchildren. She never bothered forwarding alumni mail to me. I guess the alums lost track."

"I'm not pretending Connor spent his life pining for you. There have been other women, probably many of them. My son is a professional football player. Some girls want to do the whole team I'm told. Some are fixated on special players or positions like quarterbacks. Connor is young, rich and good-looking. I don't ask about his women. But, I approved whole-heartedly of this year of celibacy. He needs to settle down with someone nice."

"Spoken like a mother," Stevie laughed.

"I will tell you he hasn't brought any of the others home to meet his family. When he called me after that game where you were injured, he said, 'Mom, I've found Stephanie Dowd,' the first words out of his mouth."

"I'm Stevie now, Stevie Dowd, sports photographer. Not Stephanie Dowd, naive college girl. I keep telling Connor that."

"You are a beautiful, independent, talented young woman who doesn't need a man to tell her anything." Mrs. Riley took Stevie's hand. "But don't let that keep you from believing someone could love you at first sight or love you forever—no matter how many men or women have been between you."

"Not even a brother?"

"Not even a brother." Mrs. Riley smiled.

Footsteps thumped up the stairs. A head of dark curls poked through the doorway. Katie Riley said, "Granny, cab's here. Granddad says let's get moving before Colby wets his pants again."

Kristen Riley laughed. "I am being summoned. Won't you come with us?"

"Really, I'd like to pass. I promise I'll spend the day with the family tomorrow."

"If you're sure."

The downstairs noise increased with multiple door slammings and Merrilee's voice inquiring if Kevin had the diaper bag and Cammie's baby doll.

"Hurry up, Kris," Keith Riley shouted up the stairs. "Let's get this circus on the road."

Kristen Riley moved out of the room to join her family and left Stevie with the solitude to think.

****

Stevie wandered down to the kitchen to check out the contents of the refrigerator, which was stocked for a family traveling with small children. It held a gallon of whole milk, a quart of orange juice, two six-packs of juice boxes, grape jelly, sandwich fixings, and an entire flat of enormous cinnamon buns obviously destined for tomorrow's breakfast. Grocery bags on the counter contained peanut butter, canned soup, a carrier of microbrewery bottled beer and a plastic sack of white bread.

Stevie heated a can of chicken soup containing pasta shaped like little stars and made half a ham sandwich on white. She threw on a denim jacket, then poured orange juice into a plastic cup. Balancing her meal on an upscale plastic plate with a pattern of sunflowers, she went outside to watch the early sunset over the bay. An inviting bench sat positioned near the water for that exact purpose. She ate her simple meal as the sky turned that deep pre-darkness blue and Venus, bright and low in the sky, appeared as if by magic. Sea birds settled for the night on the surface of the bay, and all was still and calm for minutes before night fell.

She heard the heavy tread on the boardwalk and knew by the sound of his footsteps that Connor had arrived. Bad enough she recognized his stride and worse for her that her heart beat faster. Stevie held herself back from calling out to him as he pounded on the door.

"Anybody home! It's Uncle Connor," he announced expecting to hear small children race for the door. She sighed before she could stop herself. That sigh summoned him to the bench. For a big man, he crossed the boards quickly, raised her hair in his hands and kissed the nape of her neck. She shivered.

"Chilly out here." He slid up against her on the bench and hooked an arm around her shoulders. "Where's the gang?" Ordinary words, but he looked at Stevie as if she had hung that evening star in the sky.

"Gone for fish and chips. I wasn't very hungry. I had a long flight. Too tired to go out." Stevie feared she looked back at Connor in the same way. She turned her head toward the water.

"Coach let us out for awhile, but we have a curfew just like college. All meals to be taken together, building team togetherness, you know the drill."

"More likely keeping all of you out of bars and away from bad women."

"If I know Joe Dean, a few minutes are all he needs to find bad women, but I hear he gave game tickets to that model, Amber, and told her to bring a friend. I think they are shacked up at the same hotel as the team, so he won't have to go looking and can save his energy for the game."

"What about you? Are you saving your energy

for the game?"

"What do you think?

Connor opened her coat and slid his hands under her T-shirt and up her torso to do a quick release on her front-hooked bra. His cool fingers slid over her warm, smooth breasts. He moved in for a kiss. His tongue delved deep into her mouth. Chaos erupted.

Small children sprinted down the deck, spotted their uncle and charged over to the bench. Stevie took a kick in the stomach from a small sneaker as Cameron climbed up on Connor's lap. Collin attacked from behind trying to scale the broad shoulders while Katherine took a lady-like seat on the bench and snuggled into her uncle's side. Colby nearly toddled into the water, but Connor stretched out his long legs and scissored him back to safety.

Cammie had a complaint. "You feel all hard and lumpy, Uncle Connor."

"Yeah, I probably do." He stood up, children dropping off of him like ripe fruit from a very tall tree. He did a few toe touches and stretched a couple of times. Pulling Stevie into the group, Connor headed back toward where the rest of the family stood chuckling over the scene.

Cammie squealed to her grandmother, "Uncle Connor was kissing that lady."

The more observant Katherine added, "He had his hands under her shirt."

Kevin Riley stepped in. "It isn't nice to tattle. Let's get inside before someone ends up in the water. We brought dessert home, remember?"

Morriloo held up a sack holding pints of hand-packed ice cream. The children swarmed around the queen bee and followed her into the house. The senior Rileys, still laughing, went with them. A porch light snapped on exposing Connor's face as deep red. Stevie knew her own must be tinged pink.

"You owe me for the rescue, bro. If you ever have

kids, remember the lure of ice cream." Kevin shot his brother an envious smile as he went to join the crowd.

"Shall we go in?" Connor offered Stevie his arm. "Looks like I'll have plenty of energy for the game."

"Wait a minute." She bent forward and re-snapped her bra, pulled her T-shirt down and ran fingers through her messy hair. "Okay, I'm as ready as I'll ever be." They went inside for ice cream.

****

"We brought you a flavor called chocolate mousse, Stevie." Mrs. Riley handed her a pint and a plastic spoon. "Connor says you love chocolate mousse."

"Thanks, very thoughtful," Stevie answered, knowing she pinked up again. She gave the laughing Connor a narrow-eyed stare.

"Plain chocolate for Collin. Katie and Cammie, you share the burgundy cherry, and a scoop of vanilla with sprinkles for my big boy, Colby," Merrilee counted out as she sat Colby on a Seattle phone book to boost him to table height. "A hot fudge sundae for Mommy since I'm eating for two," she pointed out needlessly.

"Here, Con, you can share my mint chip," Kevin offered. "You still crazy about mint chip, too, Stevie?"

Connor tensed slightly as his brother sat a dish with a scoop from his carton in front of him. Merrilee handed her husband a paper napkin. "Wipe Colby's face for me, darling," she interposed.

"No, I've gone over to chocolate mousse. This is too much for me." Stevie pried a lump of chocolate ice cream out of her carton with the plastic spoon and dumped it in Connor's dish.

Mr. and Mrs. Riley shared a container of jamoca almond fudge, but they put it down to suggest a game of Pictionary. The teams divided up with Kevin, Merrilee, their two oldest children, and Keith

Riley on one side, Kris Riley, Connor, Stevie, and the two youngest children on the other. The grandparents suggested simple drawings to the children though Colby's were always a scribble. He contributed by acting out various animals, and all overlooked the cheating. The brothers, as if trying to prove something, competed ferociously with Kevin and Merrilee being the big winners. The smallest children, allowed up long after their bedtime, fell asleep on the couch, and the evening was declared to be at an end.

"Yeah, I don't want to get fined for staying out too late on game night," Connor claimed. "Wait for my cab with me, Stevie. I need a good luck kiss."

"Yuck," said Collin on his way up the stairs after giving his uncle a good luck hug.

With Connor's big arm sheltering her from the damp, Stevie strolled up to the street. "Sorry we lost at Pictionary. There's no beating a married couple when we've only known each other a few months," she apologized.

"This game didn't matter. It's the one tomorrow that counts," Connor said, shrugging it off even though losing to his brother and his wife clearly rankled a little.

"There was a lot going on back there. Merrilee hates me and Kevin keeps making allusions to our not so torrid past. Do you think he cheats on her and that's why she's so insecure?"

"I don't know. Maybe when he travels. Merrilee believes he's never forgiven her for cheating on him in college. She's real jealous. I remember Kevin coming home the night they made up. He was still seeing you at the time. He told me you were the girl of his dreams, but Merrilee would do anything, and I do mean anything, to get him back. His exact words. She failed to mention she had stopped taking her birth control pills. Old Kev fell right into the trap."

"But all those children?"

"Every time she thinks he's cheating, she comes up pregnant. She says she has rediscovered her Catholicism, but I think it's her way of controlling Kevin."

"Just so you know, I'm not Catholic, and I'm not about to have five kids or get pregnant by accident."

"I'm not Catholic, either. Mom raised us Lutheran. Dad didn't care. Any number of kids you want to have is fine with me."

"Connor, what did I just say about our being together only a few months? Hell, we've only been intimate a few weeks."

"Stevie, I want you to stay with me out at the lake. This season is over tomorrow one way or the other. I know you usually run to stay in shape. We could run together."

"Like I could keep up with you, famous wide receiver."

"I'd slow down for you, or run my laps and sprints, then come back around for you. Whatever. We could take the sailboat out or do some water skiing when the weather gets warmer. Do you like to fish? I have a cabin cruiser at the marina. We can do some deep sea fishing and sleep over out on the Gulf."

"Connor, I have a career. I have a living to earn," she answered letting some exasperation come into her voice.

"Fine. I have plenty of land. We can build you a studio near the house. We're both on the road a lot. I'll bet I could get you a permanent assignment with the Sinners."

"Great, I need a man to do that for me. Talent counts for nothing. They'd say Stevie Dowd got the job because she's Connor Riley's mistress."

"Wife. I want them to say Stevie Dowd is Connor Riley's wife—and a great photographer. Stay with me. Give us a chance, Stevie. I know what I want. You just need a little more time to see this was meant to be."

"Oh, Connor." How could she not love this man?

Stevie cupped her hands around his thick neck and pulled his head down for a kiss that maybe made the cabbie wish he had a camera so he could sell the shot to the tabloids—golden boy, Connor Riley, with some babe, kissing under a streetlight on the eve of the Super Bowl. Some babe. She twined her fingers in his long, blond curls. His great receiver hands cupped tight around her butt. Not so much as a centimeter of air between them, they were that close together.

The cabbie gave two light taps on his horn. The couple did not seem to hear. He laid on a louder blast. They sprang apart.

"You called for a cab, Mr. Riley? You are Connor Riley of the Sinners, right?"

"That's me. You sure give quick service."

"I been here five minutes already waiting for you to say your good-byes."

"Sorry. I'm a big tipper, could you wait another minute?"

"Since I'm such a big Sinners fan, sure. Do you think you could autograph a receipt—for my kids?"

"Sure thing. Stevie?" Connor turned to find her starting back to the rented house.

From a distance of a few feet, she answered him. "Connor, I've lived with two men. It doesn't work for me. They all end up lying and cheating on me or walking out or disappointing me in some way or another. I think I should go back to my own place and start working again. I'd like to keep seeing you. Then maybe...who knows?"

"I don't lie and I don't cheat. I'd rather die than disappoint you. Believe it."

Connor Riley got into his ride and slammed the door. Stevie Dowd watched him go until the cab turned the corner and shot up the hill toward the heart of the city.

Chapter Ten

A long, long day led up to game time. As Stevie promised, she passed that time with Connor's family. They embarked on a harbor tour taking them out through the locks to the rougher waters of Elliot Bay. Colby threw up his giant breakfast cinnamon bun and milk on his father's shoes and was rushed to a tiny restroom on the ship for a cleanup.

Making the best of things, Stevie took some nice panoramas of the surrounding snow-capped mountains and the Seattle skyline from the water, touristy and unexciting, but it passed the time. When the clouds covered the scenery, she shot the wind-blown Riley family standing on the bow of the ship and did some cute kid photos she thought Mrs. Riley would cherish.

The group filled an elevator to the top of the Space Needle after a long wait in line with others in town for the game. A guide reprimanded the children for racing around and around the circular space. After half an hour, they came down and headed for the Pike Street Market where the tourists were so thick the Rileys formed a human chain and walked sideways to get down the aisles. After another long wait at a restaurant, the adults ate bread bowls of clam chowder and the kids scarfed burgers and fries. Mutual exhaustion forced them back to the rental house for afternoon naps all around.

While the house lay still, Stevie quietly checked over her cameras and supplies, stocked her vest and pulled out a black Sinner's T-shirt with the red devil on the sleeve. Going braless was more comfortable when wearing the photographer's vest and she debated which way to go with herself. What were the odds she would be sacked again? None if she stayed where she belonged. The dark shirt should provide some insurance if her vest came off. Braless it was going to be. She'd take the odds she would never appear in *Sports Illustrated* again in a sweat-soaked, white top.

Stevie shrugged on the black shirt. She pulled her hair back into a tight ponytail and topped it with her Sinner's cap. She wore black jeans and good running shoes. Double checking her credentials, she went quietly to the phone, called a cab and made her escape to Seahawk Stadium.

****

Pre-game insanity already raved by the time Stevie arrived. She took a few backstage candids of the aging grunge rockers, Seattle's finest contributors to contemporary music, who would be doing the pre-game show. The group was still for the most part grungy. A photographer never knew what would have value in the years to come and snapping them passed the time until the game. The halftime show had been hyped as patriotic and inspirational, the networks not wanting to take any chances with past snafus. And not half as interesting to film, Stevie thought.

She dined lightly on a classic hot dog and diet drink while watching the opening acts. In the quiet interval while the stages were being moved and the smoke from the pyrotechnics cleared, she walked the length of the field and checked the lighting, searched out the best vantage points. She was jogging back towards the fifty-yard line when she heard the call from a row of excellent seats. "Stefania, Stefania! It is me, your Marcello!

Crowd noise covered her groan. Marcello had flown out of her life half a dozen years ago. Why did he have to reappear now? She turned toward the stands. There he stood in all his dark-eyed Italian glory, dressed, she guessed, in what he thought was appropriate attire for an American football game: black leather pants, a black silk shirt unbuttoned to mid-chest, and a brilliant red scarf that would have made any other man look gay—but not Marcello.

His black, wavy hair was slicked back; comb marks stood out like fans in a stadium. One elegant hand draped over the shoulder of Joe Dean's model girlfriend, Amber. She could imagine the quarterback's chagrin when he found out how his other ticket had been used. Marcello and Amber, a lady in red with black accents—two beautiful people who made quite a picture. Stevie snapped one as the pair smiled for her showing their straight white teeth.

"Did I not tell my friend, Amber, that Stefania would be here when she says to me Joe Dean don't give her enough attention, to come with her and be, how you say, the competition? You see us in *Sports Illustrated* together, same issue as you. I was the handsome man in the ad who gives a glass of the finest American *vino* to the lovely lady."

"Sorry, must have missed that ad," Stevie claimed. She had seen it and wondered if the man in the shadows was a more mature Marcello than the one she had known.

"Many times I say, Stefania, you can be model, too. We go to New York together, make the big time. Once I even take the pictures of her after we make love. She is beautiful, but now too old. So sad she miss her chance."

Another voice from Stevie's not too distant past sounded behind her. "I'd like to see those pictures, sport. Still got them?" Dexter Sykes leered at her, flipped the strap of Stevie's best digital camera over his head, and held it out to her.

"I took good care of it, baby. It's ready to go.

Thought you'd want it for the game."

"Yeah, thanks, Dex," Stevie answered without enthusiasm. She was happy to have the Canon back in her possession, and not so happy to be trapped between Marcello and Dexter.

"Running into more old friends?" an insinuating voice from the next row of boxed seats asked. Kevin Riley leaned towards Amber and Marcello. His sons were seated between him and Merrilee while his daughters sat by the older Rileys. Merrilee frowned in their direction. She could not hear the conversation over Colby's demands for another hot dog and Cammie's crying because Katie spilled soda over her souvenir red devil.

Like a very noisy version of a scene from the play, *No Exit,* Stevie felt trapped in a hell with all her old boyfriends and lovers and no way out. The announcer's voice swelled over the crowd noise calling for the opening of the game. The Sinners, all in black, surged into the stadium through an entry decorated to resemble the mouth of Hell. Fans in red and black roared. Connor's family cheered.

"Gotta go!" Stevie took off as fast as her running shoes would take her. She heard Marcello yelling, "You come to the party after the game, no? Amber says all the footballers will be there. We talk of old times." She pretended not to hear.

There was, of course, nothing to photograph at the moment, just huge men stretching and officials clustering for the coin toss. Dexter Sykes stayed right on her tail.

"Stevie, wait up!"

She kept jogging. Dex pulled along side.

"I've been thinking about what a great team we were. We did some fantastic shoots together. I was looking through them last week. Lots of good things there."

"We never took shoots together, Dex. When we split, you took what belonged to you and I kept what belonged to me. "

"Well, ah, I guess so. But you see, I had an offer for some of my older pictures and since that misunderstanding about the Smokey LeBlanc shot, they, um, want you to sign a release before using them. I just happen to have it here."

Dex pulled a much folded paper from a vest pocket and offered a pen that had been clipped to his collar. He gave her his appealing Jimmy Olsen look. His fine brown hair fell across his forehead and his puppy-like brown eyes filled with pleading. A couple of inches shorter than Stevie, he looked up at her, begging.

"Who are *they*, Dex?"

"*Sports Illustrated.* This is going to open whole new doors for me, Stevie. You got to sign—for old times sake. Please."

"If I sign, will you let me alone?"

"Absolutely. You won't even know Dexter Sykes is in the same stadium.

Eagerly, he presented the pen again and turned so Stevie could use his back as a hard surface. She scrawled a quick signature and handed the wrinkled and much folded page back to Dex.

"Disappear, would you?"

"See you at the after game party, Stevie?"

"Dex!"

"I'm gone."

****

As expected in any game involving the Patriots, this was a grueling match of defenses. The Sinners could hardly make a move and the Pats didn't fare much better. At the half, the score stood fourteen-seven, the Pats. A nervous and edgy Joe Dean Billodeaux had moved the ball down the field in a series of tedious short throws barely making the first downs required. His eyes seemed to search constantly for Connor Riley who was too well guarded to receive. Finally, just before the end of the second quarter, DeVon Deets shook free, caught the ball at the twenty-yard line and took it across the line. Stevie and the Sinners fans knew hope.

In a seemingly endless panorama of patriotism during half time, three American Idol winners on moveable stages belted out fervent arrangements of *God Bless America, America the Beautiful,* and *This Land is My Land* while a hundred leggy young women cavorted around them wearing sequined Uncle Sam top hats, red and white striped waistcoats and tiny blue stretch shorts. Both teams enjoyed a long rest waiting for the smoke from the fireworks to clear. Nothing Stevie wanted to photograph there.

The third quarter passed scoreless as the defensive teams continued to dominate the game. When Joe Dean was sacked holding the ball, a collective groan went up from the Sinners fans in the audience. Several young women cried, including Amber who carefully blotted her face of tears with the end of Marcello's red scarf. Stevie snapped a picture of that since there wasn't much else to shoot so far.

She'd been on the wrong side of the field to capture DeVon's touchdown, preferring to photograph Connor who had seen no action. She had taken several of the wide receiver standing still with his hands on his hips. Stevie knew she was going soft on Connor Riley. Disgusted with herself, she looked back at the stands to see Marcello reaching across Amber to shake hands with Kevin. Just below them on the floor of the stadium, Dexter Sykes fiddled with his lens. No doubt at all, the best man of the bunch played football today.

When the fourth quarter began, Stevie took up her post near the Sinners' end of the field. She waited for that special shot to come her way. When it did, her finger hit the shutter reflexively, and she wished she had never become a sports photographer.

The final minutes of the game were ticking away when Billodeaux's long, long pass sailed toward Connor Riley. The Patriots, ready for this move, had been waiting. In the last play, their defensive back covering Riley had been injured by a vicious block. A fresh young rookie named Damon Suggs went out on to the field. He stayed close to Riley, but not close enough. Connor took off with the ball, Suggs desperately trying to lessen the gap. Stevie snapped picture after picture of Connor streaking down the field, the ball held close to his body like some cherished treasure.

Suddenly, the rookie launched himself through the air in a last attempt to stop the ball carrier. He hit high at the base of Connor's neck, the two helmets cracking together with a sound that silenced the cheering stadium. Riley pitched forward, rolled over on his neck and sprawled unconscious on the field. His hands unclenched. The ball fell gently from his fingertips. Stevie's finger held the shutter down. The camera whirred again and again unable to stop capturing the horror of what happened to the man she knew she loved.

Whistles blew. Flags flew. The clock stopped. Medics came running. Teammates and trainers engulfed their fallen comrade. Stevie let her camera drop on its cord from her numb hands.

An ambulance raced up the sidelines, the sign of a severe injury. With his head stabilized, lifeless arms and legs strapped to a board, the medics placed Connor Riley on a gurney and hustled him through the rear doors of the vehicle. Its siren turned on filling the stadium with a prolonged cry.

Stevie still stood in a daze on the sidelines, her heart thumping hard beneath her camera. The ambulance exited the field. A guard approached, took her quietly by the elbow and said she had been asked to join the Riley family being taken to the hospital in a limousine. In the confines of the long, black vehicle, Mrs. Riley patted Stevie's cold hand and asked the driver to put the game on the small screens that flipped down from the ceiling.

"Connor will want to know the outcome as soon as he wakes," Kristen Riley assured the family with a bright, brave motherly smile. Subdued by adult gravity, Kevin's kids ceased whining for cartoons and snacks from the mini-bar.

Across America, million dollar commercials ran filling the time delay. Back on the air, commentator Al Harney turned to Hank Wilkes and declared, "That was a spearing incident if I ever saw one. Suggs should be thrown out of the game, out of the league in my opinion because that was no accident."

Wilkes disagreed. "An over-eager rookie error, but a sorry shame a fine player and all-around good guy like Riley has been seriously injured. We'll keep you updated on Riley's condition. For now, we only know a severe neck injury is involved. Our thoughts and prayers go out to Connor Riley and his family."

Would the announcers dare to ruin the festivities if Connor were pronounced dead?

The second sign of the severity of Riley's injury came with the penalty, half the distance to the goal. Joe Dean handed the ball off to his halfback who went over the top to score. The extra point should have been a given, but Ancient Andy, shaken and confronted by a still snarling defensive line, kicked the ball low. The pigskin, batted down, fell back on to the playing field. The Patriot fans did cheer, but with a subdued sort of joy as they watched the clock run out.

The portable stages rolled out for the trophy presentation. The defeated Sinners left the field, heads hanging. Sports reporters cornered the winning players. The Patriots' quarterback took the high road.

"We don't like to win this way," he said. "Connor, we're praying for your full recovery. We'd like to beat you fair and square in next year's Super Bowl. Get well, you hear?" Shortly thereafter, the winning quarterback was named Most Valuable Player of the game.

"That should have been Connor," Stevie murmured.

Chapter Eleven

A circle of men clustered around the television in the hospital waiting room. On screen, an unrepentant Damon Suggs boasted to a reporter, "I saved the game, man. Riley would of scored. I should be voted MVP for saving the game."

"But the Sinners did score, in large part because of the enormous penalty you cost your team," the reporter countered.

"But they was shook, man. The Sinners was shook. That's why old Andy kicked low. I did that. I saved the game." Suggs sailed beyond reproof and way above modesty.

One of the listeners slammed his hand on the coffee table causing a full carafe to slosh over. "Damn bastard is proud of what he did. Whatever happened to sportsmanship? It's all about the money now…and getting a bigger contract."

The others in his group agreed. With her stomach churning, Stevie stood in the corridor and watched Suggs brag about injuring Connor. "It's 'cause I'm tough, man. I play tough. Can't no one touch me for tough."

She sank into a chair and put her head between her knees. Her cameras, still hanging around her neck, clunked against the green linoleum floor. Mrs. Riley came to sit beside her. Keith Riley and Kevin conferred with a doctor down the hallway.

Occupying another set of chairs, Merrilee camped with all of the children. The eldest two, old enough to realize something serious had happened to their uncle, sat quietly, though Katie sniffled.

Cammie, however, begged to go home. She woke Colby who had been sleeping in the crook of his mother's arm. The small boy began to wail. Kevin turned toward the commotion.

"Merrilee, have the limo driver take you and the kids back to the house. There's nothing you can do here."

"We're part of this family, Kevin. Why should we go when she stays?" Merrilee jerked her head in Stevie's direction.

"For God's sake, go home before I remember how sick I am of your jealousy! Do you think I'm going to fuck Stevie in some supply closet while my paralyzed brother is being prepared for surgery?" Heads turned in the waiting area at Kevin's angry words.

"Paralyzed?" Stevie jumped to her feet along with Kris Riley.

"They are doing some scans. It's definitely a broken neck, but they don't believe the spinal cord is severely injured. If they can take the pressure off the cord, he may be fine. It's a wait and see proposition."

"And you want me to leave at a time like this?" Merrilee pouted.

Kevin Riley answered sharply, "He's not your husband, Merrilee," then softened his voice. "You're a good mother. The kids need to be in bed. Take them back to the house. I'll call with any news." Kevin began gathering up his family's baggage: the diaper bag, the dolly, the slightly soggy red devil toy and other souvenirs of the game. He piled them into his wife's arms, picked up Colby and took Cammie by the hand. "I'll walk you to the limo." The small procession moved towards the doors to the parking lot.

"Paralyzed?" Stevie searched the face of Keith Riley who had come over to take his wife in his arms.

"It may be only temporary, but for now, yes, from the neck down."

The three of them settled in for the eternal wait for more word. Kevin rejoined them. No one talked. The silence ended with the ringing of Stevie's cell phone. She fished it from a pocket in her vest.

"Yes, this is Stevie Dowd. I did photograph the spearing incident, but I don't know. I don't think I want to sell the pictures."

Kris Riley raised her head from her husband's shoulder. "Sell them, Stevie. Let everyone see how my son was injured. I hope Damon Suggs is barred from ever playing football again."

"I'll have to get to a computer. I can't leave the hospital right now. As soon as I can." She disconnected. The phone rang again.

"Yes, I have the shots. Sure, the whole sequence in the morning." Stevie turned off her phone. "The AP news service wants a picture. *Sports Illustrated* wants to look at all my game shots. I'll need a computer to download the pictures."

"There's one at the rental. I had a hell of a time keeping the kids off of it today. It's in the den. Do you want me to take you back there?" Kevin offered.

"No, not now. Not until we get word on Connor," she refused.

Word came in the small hours of the morning when the lights in the corridors burned low and the television in the waiting room sat silent. Nurses walked noiselessly in their white shoes and spoke in low tones. Patients slept a drugged sleep, but now and then a low moan overcame the medication.

Kris Riley, eyes closed, curled against her husband. Stevie had pulled her Sinners' cap down and tried to rest under the cover of its brim. Unable to settle, Kevin Riley paced the corridor. He first spotted the surgeon coming through the ICU doors.

"I'm Dr. Weeks. We've finished the repair on the vertebrae. The spinal cord was somewhat traumatized, but not severed or crushed. We reduced the swelling with cold treatments and that seems to have made a big difference. My team thinks the injury will heal with time. He's breathing on his own, another good sign. Mr. Riley is awake and aware now, but still a little groggy from the anesthetic. You can each have a few minutes with him. Then, I suggest you go home and rest and return during visiting hours. Just a few words to let him know you are here, then go."

The four followed the surgeon back through the ICU doors and toward one of the big, glass-walled units watched by nurses at a circular station ringed with monitors. They passed an elderly white-haired man gasping for breath with the help of an oxygen mask clamped to his face. In a second room, a young woman wept quietly by the side of an accident victim pierced with needles connected to yards of tubing.

They came to Connor's bedside where he lay braced and immobile, connected to monitors and drips. His soft blue eyes were open but blurry. Kris Riley went to his side.

"What have they done to my baby boy?" she asked, tears choking her.

"S'all right, Mom. Be fine." Connor's words came slowly.

"We know that, son. Of course you'll be fine. You'll be playing in the Super Bowl this time next year," said his father as heartily as he could manage.

"Yeah, Con. Better have a fast recovery before I decide to leave my wife and family and run off with Stevie," Kevin joked. The humor sounded awkward and out of place in the stillness of the ICU.

"Stevie?" Connor cast his eyes to the side, searching.

Stevie stepped from behind his family and took his large hand lying heavily on the edge of the bed. She raised it slightly, stroked the light, golden hair on the knuckles, rubbed the calluses on the palm made by the thwack of the football, then lowered her lips and kissed the back of hand. "I'm here, Connor."

"Stevie, go home," he said as if forcing out each word.

"Soon. We'll be back later after we've all had some rest."

"No, go back to N'Orleans, Stevie. Your old place." Connor moved his eyes from Stevie clutching his hand and stared at the ceiling.

"Connor? I don't understand." Her voice broke under the hurt.

"Can't feel that. Can't feel my hand. Go home." Connor closed his eyes as if dismissing everyone in the room. "Go home, all of you."

Chapter Twelve

Despite the worry, despite the fear, Connor Riley's loved ones slept past noon. They returned to the hospital in a group including Stevie Dowd and a petulant Merrilee who had used the morning to contact a babysitting service. Their group broke in on two other visitors and the tail end of a conversation. Joe Dean Billodeaux and Andy Mortenson sat in the small bedside chairs making the furnishings look even tinier.

"I wanted to win it for you so bad, Con. I've never missed a kick that easy in my entire career. I'm so sorry."

"We wouldn't have been at the Bowl without you, Andy, so throw away the violins and keep the golden toe in good shape for next season. Okay?"

Andy Mortenson nodded, then said, "You bet," when he realized Connor could not turn his head toward him.

Joe Dean stabbed a plastic spoon in and out of a half-cup of chocolate pudding remaining on a lunch tray shoved to one side.

"I'd like to kill that Damon Suggs." He twisted the spoon and the handle snapped.

"Nurse Nannette is going to be upset. She was planning on taking that spoon home to her son, the spoon she fed Connor Riley with," Connor said lightly.

"Is Nurse Nannette the big blonde or that cute little brunette? Maybe she's a Cajun gal, lonely, a long way from home, who could use some company from the bayou," Joe Dean inquired, his interest piqued. "Either one can spoon feed me any day."

"Neither. She's the black one who weighs about the same as you, only stands a foot shorter. That woman sure can shovel pudding whether you want it or not."

"Well now, that killed my fantasy fast, fast. I've been thinking of giving up my sex life anyhow. You know, do a celibate season like you almost did. Bet I could last all the way through the Super Bowl. You'd better be around to see the miracle."

Joe Dean squirmed on this seat. "I lit a candle for you this morning and made my promise to St. Jude. Don't have to start the celibacy thing until we're playing football together again, though. I mean, St. Jude can't make all things happen—like a whole year without sex. That would be truly impossible, at least for me." Joe Dean tossed the broken spoon into the waste can as Nurse Nannette rolled into the room.

"You have more guests, Mr. Riley, so these two have to go no matter how handsome they are, and even if they do claim to be your brothers. Out, out!" She waved the football players into the hallway and made room for the family.

Merrilee was the first to the bedside. "I wanted to stay last night, Connor, but Kevin made me take the children home."

"Sure. Thanks for coming." Connor accepted cheerful greetings from his parents and Kevin, both sides putting on a good show of confidence. Everyone in the room ignored the fact that Connor's hands and legs were strapped into place and turned their eyes from the catheter bag filling with urine through a tube.

Stevie took a deep breath and placed herself at the foot of the bed where Connor could not help but see her. He took one glance, then studied the ceiling again. "I told you to go home, Stevie. I don't want you seeing me like this."

She pulled up a chair and seated herself. Resting her arms on the bars at the foot of the bed, she answered, “Make me go home, Connor Riley, because I’m not leaving until you can.”

Merrilee gasped. “How can you be so cruel when you know he’s—you know he can’t move.”

“He will move. The sooner he focuses on that the better, Merrilee. And I’ll be here to see it.”

Nurse Nannette, back on patrol, announced, “Only two of you at a time. What say we start with the parents? The rest of you get some coffee or read a magazine in the waiting area.” She shooed Kevin, Merrilee and Stevie into the hall.

“I could use another cup of Seattle coffee. You?” Kevin nodded at both women.

“Tea for me, dear. You know how coffee upsets my stomach when I am expecting,” Merrilee said sweetly.

“Guess I forgot. Stevie, you want anything?”

“No, I’m good, Kevin. Thanks anyhow.”

“We’ll be in the waiting room, honey.”

They moved past the accident victim. The old man in the oxygen mask had gone away in the night, whether to another floor or another realm, they did not know. Kevin continued on to the elevators while Stevie and Merrilee peeled off into the deserted waiting room. Stevie flopped down in a lounger, her long legs hanging over the edge of the seat. Merrilee, however, assumed a stance with her hands on her hips and her pregnant belly thrust nearly into Stevie’s face.

“I know what you are up to.”

“Huh?”

“You couldn’t have Kevin so you stalked poor Connor until he noticed you. As if that ‘collision’ shown on television was an accident. You intentionally got in his way. Once you got your hooks into him, I’ll bet you thought you got the better deal—a rich football player instead of a hard-working engineer who is away all the time on projects."

"Connor is gone a lot."

"For half a year. The rest of the time, he leads a life of luxury."

"So?" Stevie shifted her position from lounging to upright just in case Merrilee decided to jump her.

"So now Connor isn't such a great catch. He won't be making piles of money. He won't even be making love to you. He will spend the rest of his life in a wheelchair. Sure, you can stick around and live off of him and play at being his nurse. That would be very convenient. When Kevin comes to visit his crippled brother, you'll stick out those big tits of yours and try to lure him away from me."

Stevie stood up and towered over the smaller woman. "I have no designs on Kevin. He dumped me for you. If anything, I'm relieved I didn't marry him."

"You're just saying that to shut me up. Please, I can't compete with your long legs and blonde hair and great career. I'm a wonderful mother. I stay at home with my kids. I breast-fed all of them until they turned two. My boobs look like tube socks when I'm not nursing. I have stretch marks on top of stretch marks."

"Look Merrilee, I'm pushing thirty and my tits and ass aren't nearly as high as they used to be, so don't feel bad."

"Kevin follows your career."

"He does?"

"Yes, he buys *Sports Illustrated* every week."

"Along with a couple of million other people."

"He Googled you right after you moved in with Connor."

"Probably to make sure I hadn't turned into a gold digger. He has his brother's best interests at heart."

"I'm begging you for the sake of my children, don't take Kevin away from me." Merrilee began to sniffle.

"Once more let me say I have no interest in Kevin. And Connor *will* walk again. I'm staying here until he does. I suggest if you are so worried, you take your husband home with you." Stevie balled her fists.

"Hey, what's going on in here?" Holding two steaming paper cups, Kevin Riley loomed in the doorway. He had a slight smirk on his face as if he had overheard and enjoyed two women bickering over him.

"Oh, Kevin! Stevie said the most terrible things to me." Merrilee rolled her big belly against her husband's body and buried her head in his chest. She let the tears fall. "She doesn't believe Connor will walk again. We should bring your brother back to New Orleans where people who really care about him can watch over him."

"I don't think Stevie said any such thing. Your hormones are taking over again, babe. The doctor says Connor can't be transported right now, and you know Dad and I have to get back to work. Let Stevie take care of my brother. I know she'll be great at it like she is at everything."

She was, too. The couple who owned the house on the water allowed Stevie and Mrs. Riley to stay in their guest rooms when the situation was explained to them. They'd seen the accident on television at the lodge in Snoqualmie where they'd holed up to avoid the Super Bowl congestion like New Orleanians fleeing to their wilderness camps during Mardi Gras. Renting their place more than paid for the vacation and the next month's house payment. Darin and Jennifer Ames were inclined to be generous and sympathetic, even if they were not big football fans. Still, they had heard of Connor Riley.

"The hunky one with the blond curls, right?" Jennifer guessed.

"The curls are gone for now. They had to shave

them for the surgery, but he's still a hunk. My hunk," added Stevie.

Mrs. Riley smiled at her possessiveness. And why not, Stevie thought. At the end of this tragedy, Kristen Riley might have the joy of seeing her younger son settled and possibly adding a few more grandchildren to the family, as if five weren't enough.

Not wanting to impose any longer than necessary, Kris Riley and Stevie took a short-term lease on a condo near the rehabilitation unit where Connor would be sent upon release from the hospital. They'd waved good-bye to Keith and Kevin Riley who had to get back to their business and to Merrilee and her brood at the airport as soon as Connor had been taken out of the ICU.

The doctors were satisfied with Riley's progress. They kept reminding him what a very lucky young man he was. Those strong neck muscles probably saved his life when a lesser man might have died. His prime, athletic body continued to heal rapidly, they claimed.

At this comment Connor snarled, "Then why can't I feel anything but a little prickling?" Time, the doctors said, it takes time.

He wasn't much more pleasant to his mother and Stevie. When Kris Riley gently teased him about his shaved head, he growled, "I feel like godforsaken Samson. All my strength is gone."

When Stevie asked the therapist to show her how to massage his muscles, Connor said, "I don't want you looking at me under the covers while my body turns to mush."

He wanted an aide to feed him, not Stevie, not his mother. He wasn't their damned baby.

The hospital's psychologist counseled the women that anger was not unusual and definitely better than despair. "Connor shows a fighting spirit. People who despair succumb more often to infections and side effects. The power of the human mind cannot to be underestimated."

The breakthrough came quite suddenly one morning when Mrs. Riley had gone for coffee and Stevie worked with the therapist slowly bending and pumping Connor's legs, massaging the muscles of his calves and thighs. After only a few weeks of lying immobile, Connor's muscles had softened, lost bulk. As she dug her fingers in trying to stimulate the nerves and tissues, Stevie's mind drifted. She shut out Connor's ranting for her to go home and leave him alone and went back in her mind to the last time they had made love.

She remembered the strength of his legs scissoring her more tightly against him when she rode on top, their endurance when he pumped into her. She shut her eyes as she stroked up and down his thigh. Something soft but growing harder bumped against her hand. Stevie opened her eyes and looked, not at Connor, but at the therapist, sturdy, no-nonsense Mrs. Jessup, who days ago had prompted Stevie to call her Jessie.

"Jessie?" she questioned.

"Oh, that happens. That part of the body doesn't seem to be connected to the other parts in men. It has a mind all its own. The will to survive, I guess. Those who are permanently confined to wheelchairs can have sex and conceive children. An erection must hurt with a catheter in, though."

"Don't talk about me like I'm not in the room," Connor snapped. "Stevie, stop whatever you are doing down there. What if my mother walks in?"

"I'm only massaging your leg. This one," she said poking him hard in the calf.

"Hey, that hurts. Quit it. You had impure thoughts showing all over your face. You looked like you were going to come any min—"

Stevie pinched. His leg jerked. Connor stopped complaining. "Stevie," he said quietly, "It hurts. It really hurts."

All the tears she had not cried for him while trying to be strong wanted to come out at once. She bent over the hellacious gear keeping his neck and head immobilized and kissed Connor Riley on the lips, the cheeks, his closed eyes. "Oh, Connor!"

Connor gave his mother a small wave of the fingers when she entered the room. Mrs. Riley dropped the paper coffee cups and started crying as she stood in a spreading puddle of hot mocha. Stevie took credit for all of the tears she mopped from his face, but she suspected some of them belonged to Connor.

"Can you move your toes, Mr. Riley? That's great. I see your fingers are working a bit, too," Jessie observed. "Good, good. Progress will come fast now, but remember, you still have to stay immobile until that neck heals. Now, you'll be able to help us exercise these legs so it won't be so much work for Stevie and me."

"Yeah, you two-hundred pound side of beef. You can move your own legs from now on." Stevie tried to sound tough, but her voice wavered. She felt another tide of tears rising.

Forgetting his mother's presence, Connor smiled up at Stevie. "Hmmmm, sex in a wheelchair. Why Miss Jessie, I think you are putting ideas into my head. One other thing, though. Could you take the catheter out? It's damned uncomfortable."

Chapter Thirteen

Progress came swiftly, but not swift enough for Connor Riley. He stopped telling Stevie to go home and started haranguing his doctors to allow him to return to New Orleans. The doctors retorted that Seattle had some of the best medical facilities in the world and he was a lucky man to have been incapacitated here. They held him for eight interminable weeks until everyone from the neurosurgeon to the physical therapist made certain their patient could travel. Once out of the head and neck brace, Connor took his first steps held up by two sturdy male nurses with Mrs. Jessup looking on.

"You've lost weight and muscle mass, Mr. Riley. Keep that in mind. Go slowly. Sit down when you must, and for God's sake, don't fall trying to be independent."

"Yes, ma'am...Miss Jessie." Connor stooped and gave his middle-aged therapist a peck on the cheek. She blushed. He looked at the two male nurses. "For you guys, I got nothing."

Laughter felt wonderful to him. Trying to comb back his bristly blond hair was a hoot. Holding Stevie to his chest and feeling her warmth against him outranked feeding himself and using a urinal ten to one on the fabulous scale. They would go home together and make love again. Of that, he was certain.

The day Connor Riley returned to New Orleans did not pass without its little humiliations, however. His mother insisted on calling in a hair stylist to do something with his chopped locks.

"You know there will be cameras, Connor. There always are around you. Just relax and let Mr. Brice give you a new look," Kris Riley fussed.

Unable to resist, Stevie photographed the ordeal, capturing every grimace as Mr. Brice evened, moussed and mussed Connor's hair into standing up in pricks on the top of his head. The hairdresser waxed eloquent over working with a natural blond who had wonderful texture and built-in highlights. He knew Stevie's color photography would pick up the red in his face from neck to scalp. She got a good shot of his expression of horror when he looked in the mirror, too.

"I look like a marine gone gay," he groused.

Deeply offended, Mr. Brice pouted. The hairdresser recovered when Mrs. Riley escorted him into the hall to hand over his check, plus a mighty tip, and add an apology for the all the trouble and the insult.

Back in the room, Connor said loudly to Stevie, "I'd rather look just like a marine—or a football player, okay?"

The wardrobe he chose to wear home consisted of new running shoes, black jeans, a black turtleneck with a high collar to cover the marks of surgery and a black Sinners jacket that would be way too warm back in New Orleans. He tried to talk Stevie out of her Sinners cap, but Kris Riley whisked it away before her son could smash the hat down on his head and wreck his new do.

Riding out to the cab in the wheelchair rubbed against the grain of Connor Riley, but he understood rules had to be followed. He gave Miss Jessie a smacker that left her blushing again and a grin and a wave to the rest of the staff who had formed an entourage behind the chair wheeled by his mother. Stevie brought up the rear without complaint hauling a duffel bag of get-well cards and letters, red devils—handmade and store-bought in cloth, clay, and china, one knitted by a granny in a nursing home—and hundreds of other tokens of luck and good wishes from fans and teammates that had blanketed the walls of his room.

Connor caused some trouble at the airport when he refused another wheelchair ride and disappointed many aides in waiting, but his mother diplomatically asked for a motorized cart for the three of them to negotiate the crowds. A well-meaning stewardess, who obviously cared nothing for football, made the situation worse as the three settled into the wide, comfortable seats in first-class by asking pleasantly if Connor was a big Sinners fan on the way to a game.

"I play for the Sinners, and it's the off-season, lady," he said through gritted teeth. As the flight attendant scurried off to bring him an orange juice, Connor turned to Stevie and asked, "Do I look that bad, that strange to people?"

Stevie considered the question by making an imaginary lens with her fingers and focusing on Connor. "It's the hair. People remember you as Goldilocks. And you are thinner. Those great Viking cheekbones are standing out. Marcello would say you have wonderful potential as a male model."

"Why doesn't that make me feel better?" He snatched his orange juice from the attendant.

"I'm so sorry I didn't recognize you, Mr. Riley," she fluttered.

The woman was attractively over thirty, very slim, nicely made up, and obviously knew a hundred complex ways to tie scarves and placate passengers as part of her job.

The attendant went on, "The man two seats behind you says you are quite famous and wonders if you would autograph his cocktail napkin—for his son, of course. I don't follow football very much, but I'll be looking for you this fall now that I know who you are. Do you live in New Orleans?"

"Mandeville," Connor mumbled as he signed the napkin. Like a man used to sleeping on planes or one just out of a long convalescence, Connor closed his eyes and slipped into sleep as easily as he evaded defensive players.

Stevie exhaled. If she had been sitting with Joe Dean, he would have peeled off a corner of the napkin and gotten the attendant's phone number by now, but not her Connor Riley.

****

Connor woke grouchy, his neck sore and stiff despite the pillow provided, as they landed in the Big Easy. The stewardess made sure they were the first off the plane, just as Kris Riley had made sure another cart would be waiting to take them up the concourse as the three emerged from the warm humidity of the connecting gate into the chilled air of the terminal. They approached a security area gridlocked with people in red and black and dominated by big men in team jackets. The Sinners had turned out for the homecoming of their fallen hero.

The team formed an escort through the crowd toward the waiting limousine allowing Connor to sit back, wave and smile like the queen of England in a glass coach. Reporters shouted out questions. "How you feeling, Connor? You going to play again?"

"Feeling great. Nothing can stop me now," he answered ambiguously.

Joe Dean Billodeaux, trotting along side of the cart said, "Man, oh, man, what did those doctors do to your hair, boy? You look like some French Quarter faggot."

"If I had a helmet, I'd be wearing it now. It's good to be back."

In an undertone, Joe Dean asked, "You *are* going to play again, right? I mean I got this promise to St. Jude to keep if you do. I don't have to start the celibacy thing until the regular season, right?

Exhibition games don't count, do you think?"

Quietly so that neither his mother nor Stevie who sat behind him could hear, Connor answered in a whisper, "Damn right, I'm going to play again. I think you should start the celibacy thing right now to be extra sure that happens."

Joe laughed nervously. "You're kidding, no?"

At the limo, Coach Buck leaned over his star player and patted him gently on the shoulder. "Good to have you home, son. We'll take it easy and see how it goes."

Those words of kindness worried Connor through the heavy I-10 traffic and across the twin spans over Lake Ponchartrain clear to his own gateway off the tar road running between the pines. His mother and Stevie kept up a happy chatter during the ride that let him rest after the fuss of his return, but he kept thinking Coach should have slapped him on the back and said he'd be seeing him at training camp.

Eula Mae and her mother waited for him. "We got your favorite chocolate mousse in the refrigerator, Mr. Connor. Looks like you could stand some feeding up."

"I think I'm off of mousse and pudding for awhile, ladies. On second thought, don't throw it out. No sense wasting good mousse."

They laughed wickedly in the way of servants who also changed his sheets. "Good to have you home, sir. Been right dull without you," Eula Mae assured him.

Kris Riley stayed long enough to make sure her son had a good dinner and to prompt him to get to bed early. Tactfully, she did not give Stevie the same advice, but left them together with a promise that the whole family would be by to visit tomorrow.

"You heard Mom, Stevie. Early to bed." He steered her toward his room.

"Are you sure you want me with you tonight,

Connor?"

Now Stevie was treating him like an invalid, too. "I can't promise much tonight, but I'd be happy for the company."

Stevie gave him one of her softest smiles, the kind that came accompanied with tears. He hurried her to bed before that could happen.

****

Connor, regretting that all they had done last night *was* sleep, left Stevie dozing under the sheets. The Sinners organization had promised to send a car for him early and it soon arrived. Their staff of professional trainers, therapists and kinesiologists waited to begin what would undoubtedly be weeks of pain and torture needed to bring Connor Riley back into playing condition. He braced for it as a necessary part of playing the game.

Joe Dean came to watch Connor work out. With a fat magazine tucked under one arm, the quarterback leaned against a piece of weight equipment and observed an exercise amounting to having Connor turn his head from side to side a little farther than felt comfortable. While the motion wasn't exactly strenuous, beads of sweat formed on his forehead as if he were lifting weights. As his head swung towards Joe Dean, he grunted, "What are you doing in the city during off-season?"

"Oh, I came on down for your homecoming. Thought I could catch up with Amber, the model, while I was in town, but she's gone off with that I-talian dude Stevie used to—" Joe Dean paused, taking in the grim expression on Connor's face. "Used to know. He's taking her to see Rome. What she really wanted to see was Chapelle, but I don't take 'em home to my mama, you know."

"I know."

"I guess Stevie and your mama got pretty close these last few weeks."

"Yep."

"I'll bet they didn't get you the *Sports Illustrated* swimsuit issue to look at while they hovered over your sickbed."

"Nope. Stevie got recorded books. She wanted to share her favorite classics with me while I couldn't get up. Would you believe *Tale of Two Cities,* unabridged?"

"That's what a sucker like you does for love. What I did for friendship is save you several copies of selected back issues, the one of Suggs doing the spear that Stevie caught on film. It cost him one hell of a fine and the Pats are going to trade him. You can take a look at it whenever you need to raise your aggression level. That was no accident."

"Figured."

"And I bought multiple copies of the swimsuit issue. I thought you'd want to save some for your grandchildren." Joe Dean went over to the wall closest to Connor's face, took a roll of tape from his shirt pocket and pulled a few pages out of the magazine he carried. He fastened some pinups to the wall at Connor's eye level. When Connor's head swung back that way, it stopped with a jerk.

"Damn you, Billodeaux, I could have hurt myself. Why didn't you just tell me Stevie was in it?" Connor's eyes roved over the body of a younger Stevie Dowd. The full-page photo taken on some tropical beach showed an overhead shot of the woman he loved clothed mostly in sand, a small dune covering her pubic area, her breasts coated with fine, white particles. Her eyes closed, her mouth slightly open, her hair wet and tangled, he recognized the ecstatic pose from his own bedroom. If she wore a bathing suit, Connor failed to see it.

"Damn," Connor said again in a breathless way.

A second shot portrayed Stevie from the back. She looked out at an azure sea. Her hands held her wet hair up off her naked back. The eye was drawn down the lovely violin shape of her body to where the crack in her behind cheeks began. The crack showed slightly visible above a tiny turquoise bikini bottom. Connor's eyes continued down her long legs to her ankles buried in soft, white sand.

In the third photo, Stevie posed in the crotch of two palm trees growing in a V-shape. Her legs rested on one trunk, her back against another, while her arms clutched the rough trunk above her head. Both her bottom and breasts were barely covered by the turquoise bikini. Somehow, Connor felt disappointed more didn't show.

He slowly turned his head again, back and forth, without comment.

"The photo credits go to Dexter Sykes in case you want to beat him up or something. I'd be happy to help you," Joe Dean offered magnanimously.

"Can't kill a man for creating a thing of beauty, Joe. Bring all your extra copies over to my place tonight. I don't want you slobbering over Stevie while Amber is out of town."

"Done. I'll see if I can find some nice redfish to grill with peppers and onions."

"Sounds good. Better than that hospital crap I've been eating."

"Billodeaux!" came a shout from the trainer who had been working on some bad knees at the other end of the gym. "Get your ass out of here and stop distracting my patient."

"I'm a gone pecan." Joe Dean winked at Connor as he walked out.

****

To Stevie, Connor seemed exhausted, but he sat with a cold beer in one hand and watched with good humor as Joe Dean forked over hot dogs to Kevin's children and served grilled redfish fillets sprinkled with Cajun seasoning and nested in sautéed green peppers and onions to the adults. The kids wolfed their food and ran riotously over the lawn. They called to Uncle Connor to come play football with them.

Connor shook his head and took another piece of garlic bread from the basket. “Not tonight, guys. They worked me too hard today.”

Stevie looked over at Kris Riley who sat across the table from her. Connor’s mother whispered. “He’s eating well.” Stevie nodded, swallowing her concern along with a gulp of a nice, crisp white wine.

“Let me turn off the grill and I’ll take you on,” Joe Dean offered. He caught the small purple and gold LSU football Collin tossed to him and charged after the children.

Merrilee, bulging in the last month of her pregnancy, rested her hands on her stomach and burped genteelly behind her hand. “He must have been a hyperactive child.”

“No doubt,” agreed Kris Riley.

“He told me he had ten nephews and nieces from his four married sisters so I can understand why he’s good with kids. He can cook. From all the women who pursue him, I bet he has no trouble in the sex department. Why isn’t this man married?” added Stevie.

“He wants to follow in Joe Namath’s footsteps and marry when he’s forty, I think. He’ll settle down when he’s too old to play, he told me once,” Connor replied. He yawned.

“Maybe we should declare this evening over,” Stevie suggested.

Merrilee frowned. “You’ve had Connor all to yourself for months. How about giving us some time? We were very worried about him.”

“Hey, I’m fine. Let the kids play awhile and give Joe Dean some exercise,” Connor insisted.

They ended the evening with ice cream sundaes. Joe Dean was the last to leave. He sat provocatively licking chocolate syrup off of his spoon while Connor walked the family to their cars and helped pack the children into their seats.

"Connor show you the swimsuit issue?" he asked Stevie.

"Yes," she said tersely.

"You got nothing to be ashamed of. From what I saw, you were right up there with the rest of the models."

"Four years ago. Look, Dex and I took a vacation to Mexico. We rented one of those rubber boats and found a secluded beach for a picnic. He wanted to try his hand at that kind of photography. I wanted to help him out. After all, I took skin shots of Marcello for his modeling portfolio. It was business. He never showed the pictures to anyone as far as I knew…until now. I could kill him for taking advantage of me and Connor. Did you see the caption? *Photographer Stevie Dowd, who took the riveting pictures of the Super Bowl spearing incident injuring Connor Riley, performs just as well on the other end of the camera.* Now I know what those release forms were that Dex was so eager to get me to sign."

"Hey, Connor is cool with it. He probably likes thinking he has you and no other man does. You done any, ah…you two been intimate since he got out of the hospital?" Joe Dean wiggled his dark eyebrows and grinned suggestively. He licked his spoon again.

"No. He can't possibly be ready for that yet."

"Well, sugar, don't let it wait too long. A man needs to have self-confidence to play and having sex is one thing that gives it to you. I can swear to that."

"But Connor won't play again, I'm sure. How can he after an injury like that?" Stevie asked.

"Stevie girl, why do you think all the trainers and therapists are swarming all over Connor? It's not just because they want to help. Connor Riley, unlike me, was a first-round draft pick, and he stayed with the Sinners for big bucks when he could have gone free agent. He is a high-priced investment, and they'll have to pay out his contract whether he plays or not. He'll be back on the field come fall."

"No. Impossible." Stevie denied what she heard. "He could die or be paralyzed."

"Mark my words, Stevie Dowd, Connor Riley will play again. I took an oath to St. Jude that I'm already beginning to regret the closer the season gets to guarantee that."

"I don't think I can bear it if he does."

"No way to stop him."

"I can try," she answered, making a vow of her own.

Chapter Fourteen

He and Stevie were out of sync, Connor thought. Though if he stopped dozing off in the Jacuzzi or falling asleep when she massaged the sore muscles inflicted on him by the trainers, things might be different. By the time he woke up with a hard-on, Stevie had tucked herself in for the night. She often wore the turquoise tank suit she considered saggy and unflattering, but always reminded him of the first time they had been together. She slept in the guest bedroom unless he was awake enough to ask her to stay by his side.

Hell, they'd eaten the chocolate mousse out of the bowl using spoons in the kitchen. When Stevie offered him some on her spoon tip, he'd turned his face aside because her action caused a major hospital stay flashback. He should have scooped some mousse onto his finger and let her lick it off. As his flaccid muscles regained their strength, he knew he had to take charge before Stevie thought of herself as his nurse, not his lover.

When the Rev called to let him in on some news, Connor asked him to visit. "And bring that lady doctor you are so in love with," he added.

"Trouble with Stevie?" asked the Rev.

"Yep. She needs some medical advice, I think, so bring the doc with you."

The couple drove down on a Sunday afternoon, a day of rest for Connor from the torment of therapists, and shared their good tidings as they sat on the deck overlooking the lake.

"Number one, I got my fine self traded to the

Sinners to beef up that pitiful defense they got," the Rev bragged.

"You mean the pitiful defense that almost won a Super Bowl?" Connor fired back. "You just wanted a chance at a ring yourself."

"Naw, I missed my mama's cooking and my Mintay, but the money offer wasn't bad neither."

"Either, Rev. I was there the night your mother chewed you out for doing the ghetto speak all the time. She said to him, 'Revelation Jeremiah Bullock, you have a college education and a retired English teacher for a mother. Please speak correctly.'" Dr. Arminta Green gave an unprofessional giggle.

"Aw, Mintay, the other boys will beat me up if I don't talk cool. That's what I always told my mama when I was a kid." The Rev grinned back at his lady love.

Dr. Green, a slim café-au-lait-colored woman, wore her light brown hair parted in the middle, ends turned under at the chin line, a no nonsense, practical do for a busy doctor, and one that framed the fine heart-shape of her face beautifully. The small gold hoops in her ears were tasteful and not likely to get in her way when examining a patient, but they also showed off her small ears lying close against her skull and accented her skin tone well.

Mintay's green eyes were startling and unexpected beneath her dark lashes. Fine-boned, high-cheeked, and classy, it would have taken three of her to make up the bulk of the Rev. Today instead of white, the doctor dressed in a coral-colored knit top, khaki slacks and sandals with a pattern of colorful beads drawing attention to her long toes and polished nails.

"She's as bossy as my mama but can't fry a chicken." The Rev continued to smile wide and toothy.

"As if I would ever fry anything for you," Dr. Green retorted.

"She's been working on my mama, too. Now her greens taste—well—green without the fatback. Lard was my mama's cooking secret, and Mintay's done taken that away." The Rev sighed. "I dropped ten pounds in the last month. I keep telling her being big is part of my job. I have to make sure the Sinners get their money's worth."

"By the pound?" Arminta asked sharply. "I probably added ten years to your life by converting your mother away from lard."

Connor held up a hand for peace. "Rev, you know you pack it on during the off-season eating your mama's cooking, and the trainers will make sure you lose the extra during camp. Today's menu is barbecued chicken, a big salad—with croutons, Rev—and baked potatoes without sour cream. Tell Stevie the rest of your news."

"Dr. Arminta Green has consented to be my wife." The Rev picked up his fiancée's slim hand and engulfed it with his. "We're going into the city tomorrow to pick out a ring."

"I caught him off-guard. He's been asking me at least twice a month since we met in December. Being a professional football player, I figured he just wanted to get in my pants," Arminta explained.

"Aw no, honey. I never asked another woman to be my bride. You gotta know that. Besides, I'm marrying a doctor. My mama is so proud."

"The man gave up lard for me. When he signed that contract to come home to Louisiana to give us more time together, well, I had to say yes." Dr. Green extended an arm that barely reached around the Rev's shoulders to give her man a hug. He enfolded her in his huge arms and pulled her close. They exchanged a kiss for a few seconds too long.

Connor began to feel envious—and horny. He interrupted their clinch. "Say, Rev, did you see the pictures of Stevie in the swimsuit issue? I got that Sykes guy to send me poster-sized enlargements."

"You didn't!" Stevie gasped.

"Did," said Connor. "Come inside and let me show them to you. The ladies can stay out here and talk about rings and things." He gave the Rev a significant nod and led the way into the house.

Not too subtly, Connor was leaving her alone with the doctor. Still, embarrassed, Stevie hurried to explain about the cheesecake pictures. "Those were taken years ago. I turn thirty in November. You know I don't have the same body now, Dr. Green."

"Please call me Arminta, or even Mintay. I guess I'm stuck with that nickname forever now. I don't think Connor is making comparisons. He's proud of you, and I'd say in love with you."

Stevie looked out over the lake and let her eyes follow a sailboat being pushed along by the kind of breeze that would bring in thunderstorms later in the afternoon. Late May temperatures in the high eighties built clouds on the horizon.

"You don't feel the same way?" Dr. Green pressed.

"It's not that I don't. I have a poor track record with men. They either leave me, or as in the last case, I throw them out. And you said yourself, a professional football player, how good a risk is that?"

"There are exceptions. I'm marrying one."

"Connor is exceptional, too. I think he is the best man I have ever known—fond of his family, honest, good-natured when he's not hurting, courageous and loyal. I'm afraid all that courage and loyalty might be reserved for football. How can I get deeply involved with him again when I don't believe I can stand to watch him play after this injury?"

"Yet here you are. You must care for him."

"I do."

"Stevie, I know cases of professional skiers who have had injuries like this, healed, gone right back to their sport and performed well. They have the kind of personalities that won't let them give up or back down. Playing again is something Connor probably has to do for himself. Taking a chance on Connor Riley is something you have to do. A little sex isn't going to hurt him and it might help. All those good hormones rushing around, you know."

Doctor Green paused. She watched a powerful ski boat pass leaving a milky wake behind. Her mind went elsewhere for a moment. She took a large swallow from the chilled glass of white wine she held.

"Is this about sex or about love?" Stevie caught the doctor's attention again. "Because I might have had this same conversation with a certain quarterback not too long ago. Did Connor put you up to this?"

"Rev asked me to reassure you about Connor's injuries and his feelings towards you. I couldn't help but notice Connor Riley is a big, handsome man. If he wanted sex he could take it or go out and find it fairly easily. He could make a call and have it delivered. If he takes the time to set all this up with a doctor who is engaged to a football player, there is more going on than just sex, believe me."

"The problem is me, then."

"I think so. Get on with life, Stevie Dowd."

The men returned, making enough noise clomping across the wooden deck to give the women fair warning.

"Mighty fine pictures, Stevie," the Rev complimented.

"Oh, please!"

"Why don't you put on that bikini and we can all go for a swim before dinner?" he suggested. "I think Mintay wore her suit under her clothes and I brought some trunks. Connor has those little running boy hips so I knew none of his would fit me."

"Good idea," Connor said.

They had to settle for seeing Stevie in her sagging tank suit, but Dr. Green surprised the group by peeling down to a leopard print two-piece that made her small breasts and narrow hips look very tempting. The Rev picked up his fiancée without effort and tossed her off the dock. With a shout, he ran down the planking and cannonballed into the water. The splash swamped over the sides of Connor's boats.

Connor bent to pick up Stevie who started to say, "Don't hurt your—" but she was into the lake before she could finish her sentence. Then, Connor took off down the dock. Stevie, treading water next to Arminta, sucked in her breath.

"It's okay. Let the man play," Dr. Green advised.

"Pitiful, white boy. You call that a cannonball?" the Rev mocked.

"No, I call that a dive befitting the grace and speed of an exceptional wide receiver," Connor answered when he resurfaced. "I won't have to bail out the boats after doing one either."

The four splashed while the chicken halves cooked over low heat in the closed grill. By the time the Rev got a little too playful and untied Mintay's top, the meal was nearly ready. The doctor deprived him of any eye candy by swimming under water and scaling his wide back to retrieve the bikini top dangling from his thick fingers.

Connor got a quick glance of dark nipples against light brown skin, but pretended not to notice as he tamped down that envy again. He imagined how good Stevie's wet, naked breasts would feel sliding down his back and then had to stay in the water a few extra minutes worrying about the chicken being overcooked. He watched Stevie help Mintay retie her top and heaved himself out of the water to go dowse the poultry with a last minute coating of his own special barbecue sauce.

When he turned a back to the lake, Stevie called

for Mintay to put a beach towel on the edge of the dock for her. "She's afraid to come out of the water," called Connor to the Rev.

"She's afraid somebody will see," warbled the Rev like a canary singing bass. The men serenaded Stevie with an interesting version of *Yellow Polka Dot Bikini*, Connor off-key, the Rev belting it out.

"I am turning blue while you two sing. Mintay, the towel please," Stevie pleaded. The men each took an arm and hauled Stevie up onto the dock where she snatched up the towel and swathed herself in terry.

"That's one good thing about being a person of color. The blue doesn't show," Arminta laughed.

"It's not really the blue I'm worried about showing. This suit sticks to every nook and cranny."

"I love your nooks and crannies. Let's eat before my sauce burns," Connor suggested.

He'd made a barbecue sauce rich and tangy with a nip of hot pepper. His company unanimously decided he could give the Paul Newman products some competition. After dinner, the couples drank more of the white wine, dunked freshly washed strawberries into a chocolate sauce and watched the sun set redly behind a silhouette of black thunderheads across the lake. A breeze picked up taking the heat out of the day.

"Connor could do a lot of things besides sell barbecue sauce. He has a degree in mass communications his mother insisted he get and with his looks and good personality he'd be a natural sports commentator. He has the patience to coach, too," Stevie hinted.

"All great ideas for when I'm done playing football," Connor answered. "Say, why don't you guys spend the night and go into the city tomorrow?" He deftly changed the subject.

"Great sug—" the Rev began.

Dr. Arminta Green pressed firmly on his foot

with her beautifully beaded sandal.

"Great Scott! It's late. I promised Mintay we'd go to my favorite jazz club in the city tonight and ring shop in the morning. Music should be heating up about now. Been a fine afternoon, Con, but we need to get moving."

"Great Scott? When did you ever say Great Scott?" asked Connor, puzzled.

"I'm cleaning up my act since I am an engaged man. Mintay hates me using Holy Shit. So does my mama. Thanks for the offer, but we need to go. Up, up," he motioned to Arminta. She gave him a great smile.

Connor and Stevie walked them to the same black SUV that had brought Stevie to this place from her own stay in the hospital a half-year ago. It shook her to realize she had stayed with Connor longer than the Rev and Arminta had known each other. She watched the Rev hoist Mintay up, giving her a kiss on the way up to her seat. How could they be so sure so soon?

Connor's arm came around her shoulders. He waved his guests off, opening the gates with the remote for them as they approached the road. As the gates closed, he caged Stevie in his arms, tilted her head back and began a kiss as long as one of Joe Dean Billodeaux's passes.

****

Connor arched over Stevie. A drop of his sweat fell between her naked breasts as he pumped, barely aware of Stevie's nails biting into his thighs. The telephone rang, too late for casual calls or telemarketers. The long, looming storm broke over the house adding an electric energy to the night. He did not want to stop, but the bell kept pealing right next to Stevie's ear. She fumbled a hand to the receiver and raised it toward him while mouthing the words, "Don't stop."

He slowed the pace from breakneck to long and

deep. "Yeah!" he gasped as Stevie shuddered under him. "Kev? Can't hear you over the rain. Sure I can bring my SUV over. It's a nasty night to cross the causeway. Give me a little while. Babies don't just drop out, do they? No problem, I was working out a little. Couldn't sleep because of the storm. Okay, you have a dirty mind, but you'd be right. Be there soon."

Stevie groaned and bucked. Connor pitched forward and finished in a flash. He kissed Stevie as her eyes fluttered open. "You need more, my love?"

"I think I came twice while you were talking. Maybe three times. This gives a whole new meaning to telephone sex."

Connor collapsed beside her. "Merrilee is in labor. Kevin wants to borrow the SUV to take her over to Ochsner. Only the best for Merrilee. Wants me to pick up Mom on the way to his place to stay with the rest of the kids, so I guess I have to get dressed and go. Sorry."

"No apologies necessary. Here I was worrying about your hurting yourself, but I'd say you are better than ever."

"Damn right," he boasted.

She gave him a shove off the bed. "Merrilee gets between me and my man again."

"But this Riley isn't giving you up. Remember that while I'm out in the storm."

Chapter Fifteen

Merrilee's new daughter, Courtney, turned ten weeks old by the time Connor left for summer training camp leaving Stevie behind engulfed in worries. She was grateful to have a contract with *Sports Illustrated* covering the European Games. The assignment would take her mind off of Connor toiling to prove he could still play pro football. The man exuded confidence. Their sex life remained superb but her fears for him would not diminish. She secretly hoped the great Connor Riley would be cut during training or the pre-season games before anything more could happen to him. How could she be so disloyal to the dreams of the man she loved?

Stevie was not really in the mood for conversation as Kevin drove her to the airport to catch her flight to Greece. Leaving her mother-in-law behind with the older children, Merrilee insisted on coming along for the ride—and to keep an eye on her husband of course. She nursed Courtney as Kevin steered through traffic four lanes across.

"It's so nice to get out of the house. Nursing does tie you down, but I wouldn't do it any other way," Merrilee chattered on as if Stevie truly cared. "Athens, I'd love to go to Athens someday. What do you think, Kevin?"

"By the time all our kids are grown up, we'll be too old to walk up to the Parthenon," her husband answered.

"Oh, they probably have handicap transport, don't you think, Stevie?"

"Probably. I'll check it out for you." She longed

to be on the transatlantic overnight flight and away from her Louisiana problems.

"Connor called last night and said camp is going really well for him. He says it's great to be back in shape and getting ready to play," commented Kevin as he sped down the long drive to the terminal.

"Nursing helps you get in shape after giving birth, Stevie, just a friendly tip in case you and Connor ever have children," Merrilee chimed in.

"We haven't discussed it. I'm glad Connor feels so confident. Drop me at the curbside check-in. You don't have to go to the trouble of parking."

Kevin pulled over and helped Stevie get her gear from the trunk. Her final sight of the Riley family before leaving the country was of Kevin looking on with disgust as the baby released Merrilee's large red nipple with a pop that drew a glance from the sky cap.

"To think, I might have married that man," Stevie murmured as she gave a large tip to the attendant to insure her bags would arrive in Athens with her.

The trip passed uneventfully. She slept away the long transatlantic flight, got her only exercise changing planes at Heathrow and arrived in sunny, smoggy Athens with a hoard of summer tourists.

Her photography went well capturing the grace of gymnastics and its tragic spills, the power of track and field and its career ending injuries. Each mishap reminded her sharply of Connor. The blue Foto vests imprinted with a number large enough to be worn by a convict were hot and ugly and necessary for security. Guarding one's credentials in an almost paranoid manner came easily because no one entered a venue without them. Still, she delighted in being back in the game, her game, one she understood and loved despite the heat, the crazy scheduling and the demanding photo editors.

Once she dropped off her memory cards at the

warehouse serving as a press center after the final event each evening, Stevie spent the rest of her night with other photographers of many nationalities in the noisy *tavernas* of Athens. Inevitably, Connor called when things were at their rowdiest. He filled her in on his training triumphs.

"You know, I dropped some weight with the surgery and all. I'm faster than ever. It's going to be a great season," and then because she seemed to freeze whenever he mentioned playing again, he added some jokes, some small talk. "You learn any Greek yet?"

"I've learned Greeks like tall blondes and how to tell them to get lost in three languages," Stevie replied, her answer nearly drowned out by the sound of breaking glass and laughter.

"You okay?"

"Sure. Just some idiot trying to dance with a bottle on his head. Oh, it's Dex. Figures."

"Is he hitting on you?"

"Hardly. I haven't spoken to him since those swimsuit pictures came out."

"Good. Don't drink too much ouzo or you might wake up next to some hairy guy named Nick. Love you, Stevie."

Stevie looked around at her mostly male companions. "Right back at you, Connor."

Stevie felt his disappointment when she told him during the next call she had decided to re-visit Italy for a few weeks after the Games ended. "But I thought you might want to come to some of the pre-season games."

"Count me out for this year. Who knows when I'll get to Europe again," she answered breezily.

His next call caught her at a cafe off San Marco Square. When he confessed he had twisted a knee in a pre-season game and would be sitting out the next few, Stevie exhaled as if she had been holding her breath for a month. Maybe she had. Her tone brightened and she shared some amusing gossip with him, laughing over the phone. "Guess who I ran into? Amber and Marcello. She hasn't been back to the States for months. Turns out they have joined forces to form the Amberello Modeling Agency, New York—Rome—New Orleans. They gave me their card. Poor Joe. It looks like Marcello has taken his woman."

"As long as he doesn't take mine. Forget pitying Joe Dean. He's getting all the sex he can before the regular season starts. He made this crazy vow to St. Jude that he would go celibate for the season if I played again. He keeps asking me how the knee feels and if I think he can have sex while I'm on the injured list. I keep telling him he can have all the sex he wants, it's got nothing to do with me, but he's one superstitious Cajun boy."

Stevie's laughter rang out again. "I remember his worrying over the cover curse and your celibacy, too."

"Mine wasn't a vow, just a way to keep my power for the game. But, I still am celibate, since you've been gone."

The connection went silent for a moment.

"I believe you, Connor. There's no one else for me, either."

"So when are you coming home?"

"Soon, very soon."

And Stevie Dowd, sports photographer, left him hanging again. Connor stared at the phone in his hand. Not that he really was worried about Dex or Marcello or Greeks named Nick. Stevie did love him and no one else, even if she hadn't said so right out loud. Why did she hesitate to come home? So far, he'd proved he was still the same man in bed and out. The pre-season games were a piece of cake, as always. Coach played him lightly and drove the rookies to see what they had to offer. Now resting his knee, he wouldn't get on the field again until the real playing started.

Then, he could prove he was good as ever to Stevie, to Coach and maybe to himself. Deep down the great Connor Riley had his doubts, and he had to keep them there hidden in the dark away from his teammates and the woman he wanted for his wife.

****

Stevie was relieved to see her reception committee composed of the three very big men who had once clustered around her hospital bed and one slim lady doctor, not a disgruntled Kevin and a nursing Merrilee. As she passed through the security gates, Joe Dean picked her up, swung her around and gave her a big kiss on the lips while Connor looked on grinning.

"There, brother, I did you a favor by taking care of the greeting. Don't want you to put any strain on that knee now. If you need me to sub for you tonight, you call on ole Joe to come over to your place," the quarterback offered magnanimously.

"I think Stevie and I have enough imagination to handle the situation. Thanks just the same." Connor offered a welcome kiss as warm, strong and long as all the rest of him. The tenderness and intimacy of it had Mintay sighing and the Rev and Joe Dean entering the discomfort zone.

A camera flashed and Connor and Stevie broke apart. The group began to attract attention. A fan wearing a Sinners cap approached followed by two teen-aged boys. He held out a pen and an address book open to a blank page. "Could my sons and I have your autograph, Mr. Riley?"

"Do we have to pay you for it?" the younger of the boys, also dressed in Sinners gear, inquired.

Connor had already signed and passed the book on to Joe Dean. "Not a cent. I'm in an especially giving mood today." More people converged on the players.

"Look, why don't Stevie and I go down to the baggage area and get her things while you guys take care of your fans," Mintay suggested.

She and Stevie slipped through the crowd and took the escalator downstairs. On her left ring finger, Mintay wore a gorgeous estate diamond of five carats with so many facets it glittered even in the dimness of the baggage claim area.

"Love the ring," Stevie commented as they waited for the carrels to begin turning.

"Can you believe Rev wanted me to pick something larger? I told him this was gaudy enough. With washing up after patients, I won't be able to wear it all the time anyhow. To be honest, I think it's beautiful. We've set the date for March during the off-season and he's talked me into using his daddy's church for the ceremony. I do expect you and Connor to make the trip to Chapelle for the wedding, you hear," Mintay ordered.

"I wouldn't miss it for the world. Whether Connor will be with me I don't know. I can't seem to get past my fear of his playing again, and that's so unfair to him. Football is his life, I know that, but I can't bear for him to be injured again. How long do you think this knee problem will last?'

"Not long. He should be good to go for the first regular season game, Rev says. Believe me, I worry all the time, too, but their careers are short. Just hang in there."

By the time the women had hauled the bags off the beltway, the men arrived to make light work of hefting them to the Rev's Escalade. Arminta climbed into the shotgun seat and Stevie took a slot between Joe Dean and Connor. Connor put a possessive arm around her shoulder and let one big hand dangle over her breast. Even without a touch, her nipples puckered. She rejoiced that everyone else seemed to have plans for the evening. She would be alone with Connor after a two month separation.

Five minutes after waving good-bye to their friends, they stood completely naked in the bedroom. Connor fell back on the bed, arms wide, genitals flopping. Stevie, hands on her hips, posed at the foot in the V made by Connor's legs and said, "You call that ready? You call that happy to see me?"

He beckoned her with a little finger. "Gotta watch the knee so let's see what you can do on top."

Stevie looked away from the bindings around the injured knee. She straddled his hips and moved her hands to his hair. "It's nearly grown out to its old length. I missed this," she said running her fingers through the strands.

"Yeah. I think this is a good luck sign for my first game of the season. That feels good. So, no long-haired Greeks or curly-headed Italians these past two months?"

"They use too much gel. Still, I'm betting you're glad I took my birth control pills anyhow so I am right up to date tonight."

"Ummm, glad, yes."

Stevie leaned forward and rubbed her breasts delicately against the golden hair on his chest, then arced over him and offered her aroused pink nipples. He ran his hands down the long slope of her side, his fingers tickling as they brushed the edges of her breasts. He took a nipple in his mouth, suckled gently, then harder as Stevie rocked on his hips.

"Bingo," she whispered almost to herself as she rose up and came down taking all of his erection inside of her body. She moved slowly until he bucked beneath her and forced her hips to go faster. He thrust upward.

"Oh, no, you don't. You said it was my turn to be on top." Stevie continued her leisurely motions, finally taking pity and picking up the pace until they both convulsed together. After resting on his sweat-soaked chest for a few minutes, she rolled off and pulled his arm around her for warmth.

"You get to be on top as much as you want—injury or no injury. That's a promise," Connor vowed.

They fell silent for awhile, neither falling asleep. Unanswered questions hung in the air.

"Did Arminta tell you she and the Rev have set the date?"

"Of course. March. All the azaleas will be in bloom in Chapelle. Nice. Beautiful ring, too."

"It's going to be some bash. Mintay has seven bridesmaids picked out, two sisters of hers, two of his, and three cousins. He asked me to be best man."

"The only whitey in the bunch?"

"Hell, no. Joe Dean is supposed to be groomsman to the youngest of the cousins. The Rev figured that would be safe because the kid is only sixteen and Joe doesn't go for jail bait. Besides, if he gets to all the women who are waiting for him at the end of the season, he'll be too tired to come on to anyone in the wedding party."

Stevie chuckled into his chest hairs. Connor plodded on toward his goal. "Is that the kind of wedding you would want, a big splash, lots of bridesmaids?"

Stevie considered for a moment. "No, my sister did that. I'm glad she did because Dad enjoyed the party, but he's not around now to give me away. I think I'd want something simple, just family and good friends, outdoors maybe, in the spring when the weather is good or in October. October is always nice." She yawned.

"How about April? Would you marry me in April?"

"Connor Riley! Is this a proposal? Here, naked in bed after sex! No romantic dinner, no kneeling by a park bench, no computerized message on the screen in the Super Dome?"

"I can do it again tomorrow. I can do it better."

Stevie noticed the red of embarrassment creeping up his neck. "I was kidding." She kissed his cheek but did not answer his question.

"So?"

"Connor, would you give up football for me?"

"What? You can't mean that."

"I do."

Shaking Stevie from the shelter of his arm, he bolted upright in the bed. "That's not fair. What would you say if I asked you to quit photography and stay home and keep house?"

"I can't get hurt, paralyzed or dead doing sports photography. Give me your answer first, then I can give you mine."

"Untrue. If the Rev and I had hit you harder than we did, you might have ended up with severe internal injuries last year. Photographers are killed all the time in war zones."

"I promise not to volunteer for any war photography. Answer me."

"I can't give up football. Not yet. I need to prove I'm as good as ever. Better. After that, who knows how many years I have left to play? Stevie, don't do this to me. Don't make me choose."

Stevie was up, out of the bed, and searching for her clothes. She talked as she stalked around the room gathering up flung garments. "I love you. There, I've said it, and now I am going to tell you I can't stand by and watch you get injured again, maybe fatally next time. You have a house big enough for ten people, a garage holding four cars and a motorcycle, three boats, people to clean your home, tend your yard, maintain your hot tub, decorate your place for Christmas, and probably a stock portfolio ten inches thick and a million other investments because you are no dumb jock. What more do you need?"

"You." He paused for a moment. "And my self-respect. I must play. Can't you understand that?"

"No. I'm gone. I'm out of here." She yanked her shirt over her just-snapped bra, pulled her jeans up over panties inside out and stomped through the bedroom door.

Connor's bellow followed her down the hallway. "Stevie, you're always saying men walk out on you. Men disappoint you. What are you doing right now? Answer me, damn it!"

She headed for the overstuffed garage sheltering her modest car among his glossy machines, pausing only to snap up her baggage still standing inside the front doorway. She heaved her suitcase into the trunk, nestled her camera bag and the awkward folding tripod gently and punched the button to open the wide doors.

Stevie tried not to look back, but her eyes searched for one last look at Connor Riley in the rear view mirror. He stood on his portico, a bath towel tied around his waist, his broad chest pale, his long blond hair lifting in the evening breeze from the lake.

Connor raised his hand and hit the remote, opening the gates and letting Stevie Dowd go. She would be back once he proved himself on the field again. He *was* still the man she'd come to love. He would have his best season, set new records, dazzle with his speed. Then, she'd see she had nothing to fear. Stevie would not end up a widow or stuck with a cripple for the rest of her life. They had nothing to fear, nothing at all.

Chapter Sixteen

The next morning, Stevie tried to get her act together. And failed. She was amazed she had slept at all on her old sofa, now stained with a damp spot from the crying. She guessed she had jet lag to thank for the rest. So, here she sat in her own dusty and deserted place again. She had kept up the rent as a matter of pride and the studio as a matter of necessity. Connor would have built her a workroom, of course, and made it even harder to leave him. Finally home and she only wanted to get away again—as far from the situation she had created as she could.

Her mother and sister would welcome a visit. Stevie could not think of anything more depressing than being a witness to her sister's wedded bliss and happy motherhood. She could almost hear her mother saying, "Stevie, don't tell me another man walked out on you."

"No, Mom," she would answer. "I walked out on him."

She idly thumbed the pages of her address book as she sat by the phone wondering who to call. A scrap of paper stuck out from among the pages. She picked it up and read the note with a weak smile. *If you ever need a friend to protect you from all those big, bad men, call me. Jackie Haile.*

The championship golfer had scrawled a cell phone number beneath the message she left behind after the hospital visit. Stevie decided to take it for what is was, an offer of friendship, not a come-on line. She picked up her phone and punched in the number. Jackie's gruff voice answered. "Yeah?"

"Jackie, this is Stevie Dowd. I need some place to go. I need something to do."

"Man troubles?"

"Right."

"He stalking you?"

"No! Connor is the best man I've ever known."

"Explain why you want to get away from the best man you've ever known when you get here. I'm playing in Kutztown. The tour can always use another photographer, right? Heck, some of the girls drag their kids along. Maybe they need baby pictures. Whatever, come to Jackie."

"Thanks. And where is Kutztown exactly?"

"Pennsylvania. The apple butter and quilt capitol of the world, I think. It will take you three days to get here driving. You'll be in time to see me take the Wachovia Classic, a $180,000 purse, but I can't begin to tell you how to get here. Find a good map on the internet and meet me at the Berkleigh Country Club."

Stevie's phone beeped signaling an incoming call. She checked the caller ID. It flashed "Private." Connor Riley was trying to reach her. She wanted to pick up the call so badly her fingertips tingled. No, no, no.

"Jackie, I'm on my way."

****

Two days out of New Orleans on the long stretch through Virginia, Stevie's cell phone rang. A quick glance told her the number was unfamiliar. Could be Connor using someone else's phone, but after burning up her resources during the long stay in Seattle, she could not afford to ignore a possible offer of work. Stevie answered.

"Have I reached Stevie Dowd, the photographer?" a nasal female voice asked.

"Yes."

"Well, have I got an offer for you. This is

Margaret Stutes of the Sinners' publicity office. It seems we suddenly need another official photographer. You must come by my office to talk terms tomorrow."

"Thanks for the offer, Ms. Stutes, but I wouldn't be interested."

"It's a great opportunity. I need to see you right away."

"Did Connor Riley ask you to call me?"

The woman hesitated. "Actually, no. It was Joe Dean Billodeaux. Whatever our new star quarterback wants, he gets."

"I appreciate what he is trying to do, but the answer is still no. The same if Connor Riley asks you to contact me."

"Connor and Joe Dean? Girlfriend, whatever you got, I want you to boil it down, put the essence in a bottle and ship it to me express. The closest I've gotten is putting my name in Joe's little black book and with a last name like Stutes, I am way down the alphabet. He won't get to me 'til next Christmas." A heavy sigh ended Margaret's side of the conversation.

"Joe Dean might start with the Z's. Who knows? Good luck, Margaret."

"Yeah, sure. The management won't be happy with me if I don't deliver you. Could I tell them you are thinking it over?"

"Of course, but the answer will still be no. I'm on my way to cover the LPGA tour. Tell them that."

"I guess that will explain the rejection. Still, if you get back to town, drop by my office. We need to talk. The name is Margaret Stutes."

"I got it. Heavy traffic ahead. I need to hang up. Bye, Margaret." Stevie disconnected and kept on driving toward Pennsylvania.

****

Springfield, Tulsa, Portland, Sacramento and North Augusta, because Augusta would not have the women golfers, Stevie let the places she had been run through her mind. September had gone and the finest month for football played outdoors arrived, October with its bright blue weather, as the poet said. She had been to the west coast and back only to arrive at a place putting her in driving distance of Atlanta where the Sinners played the Falcons that afternoon.

The television sets in the bar at Mount Vintage were tuned to the football game. Men married to women on the golf tour had done their duty and walked the course behind their money-earning wives. Some only joined them for the weekend and went back to their jobs on Monday. Others toured with their spouses. All watched a man's game now.

In the restaurant nearby, Stevie took pictures of Connie Parks, her husband and twin daughters who were celebrating both a first place victory in the tournament and the girls' first birthday. Connie said today she could not lose. Photographs by Stevie Dowd memorialized the events.

Now sitting at the bar, Stevie pushed aside her empty glass. The young bartender, who had been getting progressively more friendly asked if she wanted another. She nodded. He fixed her up and mixed in a big smile. Jackie Haile strode across the room fresh from the showers and seized the stool next to Stevie.

Giving her a squeeze with one arm and hoisting Stevie's drink with the other, Jackie declared, "Just what I need, a long, tall ice cold drink." Jackie took a gulp, coughed, set the glass down slopping some over the edges. "Not iced tea then. Got quite a kick."

"Long Island Iced Tea with no tea in it, but it's got vodka, rum, tequila and I forget what else," Stevie recited. "Great stuff."

"Coca-Cola," the bartender added. "Can I get you something, sir, er—ma'am?" he asked Jackie as he took note of the small, hard breasts beneath the Izod golf shirt.

"Another one of those." She slicked back her short wet hair with a hand. "Damn, no wonder I lost. I forgot to put in my lucky earrings, the classy ones made like little gold knots you gave me last time I had a big win."

"Hit me again," Stevie said finishing off her third without taking her eyes from the TV screen.

"Babe, you shouldn't be watching this. Remember you said out on the west coast you were glad they didn't show the Sinners' games. I'll ask the barkeep to turn it off."

"No, don't. Jackie, I cheated. I watched the ESPN news Sundays in Portland and Sacramento. I have to know if he's been hurt."

A cheer went up from a group of Louisiana tourists. Connor Riley caught another of Billodeaux's long passes and headed for the goal line again. The Falcons fans looked glum and with a score of 10-28 Sinners, they had a right to be.

The bartender, a little less friendly than before Jackie's arrival, set another Long Island Iced Tea in front of Stevie and shoved one toward her companion. "You must be a Falcons' fan."

Stevie shook her head no. She glugged down half of her tall drink. "Sh-Sinner," she mumbled, her tongue stumbling numbly.

"Here, let me pay for this and her tab, too." Jackie held out two twenties.

"No. I pay my own way, Jackie." Stevie fumbled in her vest for cash.

"You give that football player as hard a time as you give me? Won't let me buy you a drink, a meal, a room or a plane ticket even with all the luck you've brought me."

Jackie watched Connor gallop into the end zone with nary another player near him. "Of course, that $180,000 pot I took at Berkleigh and the State Farm purse are nothing compared to what your former boyfriend makes."

"Yeah, I gave him a hard time, but I'm fine, jush fine. *Golf* magazine wants me. Even *Sports Illushrated* needs a picture of Connie and the twins and her big win. I'm doing fine all by myself. All alone." Stevie watched Ancient Andy come out and make the extra point. The clock ran out. Game over. The commercials rolled.

"But what really gripes me is coming in second to a woman who gave birth to twins last year. She should stay home with her kids, don't you think?" Jackie joked.

Stevie nursed the remainder of her drink and waited for the beer ad to end. There he was, Connor Riley with a microphone being shoved at him by a sports reporter. He'd scored four touchdowns in one game. He would be the first interviewed.

Jackie looked at the screen. "So that's my competition, not that I'm getting anywhere with you. Friends, that's all we'll ever be. Even I can appreciate that long blond hair damp with sweat, those big baby blues, great Viking cheekbones, and all that 'aw shucks' modesty."

Up on the screen, the interview continued. "What a blowout, Connor Riley. Four TD's for you, one for Deets, and let's give some credit to Rev Bullock for an interception and two turnovers against his old team, 35 to 10. What do you have to say about your phenomenal game today?" the reporter asked.

"I've given everything to the game and this is the result," Riley answered without a smile.

"Just nine months ago, you were flat on your back, hospitalized with a broken neck. No one thought Connor Riley would play again and yet this is your best season in an outstanding career. You seem stronger, faster than ever. What do you have to say about that?"

Connor turned from the reporter and stared into

the camera. “It was the best of times, it was the worst of times.” The man who was being touted as the finest wide receiver in the league appeared grim despite the victory.

“Boned up on your classics while you were convalescing, I see. *Tale of Two Cities,* right?” the commentator said brightly.

“It was spoon fed to me along with my pudding,” Connor acknowledged, still unsmiling.

“This has got to be the best of times, then, for Connor Riley.”

Riley did not respond. He turned from the camera and the reporter, who sidled quickly over to Revelation Bullock.

“Rev, great game for you, too.”

“Yeah, man, it was a good move for me to sign with the Sinners. We giving each other just what we need.”

“And what’s that?”

“A ticket to the Super Bowl, man.” The Rev’s round brown face filled the screen. He bared a grin you could bounce sunbeams off.

Jackie finished her drink. “Well, I’ve had enough of this crap. How about you, baby doll?”

Stevie buried her face in her arms on the bar. She mumbled a few words.

“Got to pick your head up, babe. I can’t hear you.”

“Our children would have had blue eyes.” Stevie’s tears rolled down both cheeks.

“For God’s sake, I can’t stand a sloppy drunk.” Despite her comment, Jackie blotted Stevie’s face with cocktail napkins. “Can you walk?’

“I can walk,” Stevie claimed sliding from her bar stool, missing the bottom rung and falling back against the counter. “The important thing is that I cannot drive, not to Atlanta, not nowhere. Tomorrow, he’ll be back in Naw Orlins, you see.”

“Yeah. I do see. Let’s get you out of here.”

Chapter Seventeen

Joe Dean Billodeaux rang the bell at Connor's place. No answer. He pounded on the oak door. No one came. "Shit," he muttered and tried the latch. The door was unlocked. Being as noisy as possible, he moved down the hall. No one wanted to come up on Connor suddenly these days. The man might have a gun, and his temper had gone off the charts lately.

"In here, Joe," Conner called in a raspy voice.

The game tape played in the den, but no hall lights burned. Eula Mae and her mother were nowhere and the house seemed too still. Connor sat tilted back in a leather lounger, eyes on the big, flat screen dominating the far wall.

The only lights shining were the tracks that usually highlighted his trophy cases but now illuminated the two full-length posters of Stevie Dowd wearing mostly sand in one and mostly nothing in the other. The pictures hung on either side of the television screen. Certainly more exciting than watching the Sinners smash the Falcons again, but maybe not as healthy.

"Hey, man, let's get some lights on in here. My mama would say you're gonna ruin your eyes. A wide receiver with bad eyes retires early, no?" Without waiting for an answer, Joe flicked on a few more lamps and took a seat in another lounger.

Connor squinted in the brightness. "Sorry, didn't hear the bell ring. This game was a blowout, but there are still a few things we could have done better."

"Tell you what, bro. We got a bye-week coming up and we played good ball yesterday. What say we go down town? There's always some action in the Big Easy even on a Monday night." Joe waited for a positive answer. He was disappointed.

"I thought you were doing the celibacy thing so I could play ball. What is it, six weeks, and you're giving up? I held out through most of the playoffs." Connor shook his head in disgust.

"And then, along came Stevie. Hey, I can still drink and attract the babes for you. Let's go."

"Along came Stevie," Connor repeated as if he had not heard the rest of Joe's sentence.

"This is no good, man. Look, let me take down those posters. Every guy knows there is only one cure for getting over a woman. More women." Joe Dean moved towards the photos of Stevie.

"Don't touch my posters, Joe. I warn you, hands off!"

"Okay, okay, *bien*. I'm going to do you a big favor, bud. I have here Joe Dean Billodeaux's little black book just chock full of names of willing women who I can't satisfy right now because of my vow. Every time one comes on to me, I whip out my book and say, 'Sugar, I made an oath to stay celibate for the season, but you put your name and number in Joe Dean's book and he will get back to you come spring.' Good for me spring comes early in Louisiana." With a big grin, Joe tossed the address book to Connor.

"Not interested." Connor tossed it back.

"Come on. I gar-run-tee you me, there is not one dog in the pack. All lovely ladies who don't know a quarterback from a wide receiver. They only want to sleep with a football player. We can perpetrate a kind of quarterback sneak on them. What do you say?" Joe threw Connor an encouraging look accompanied by a little grimace to show it hurt a little to make the offer.

"Joe, the Rev said I'm grieving, and I got to get over Stevie in my own way. This is my way."

"The Rev also said you shouldn't be alone during your time of trial. So, I'm here for you, bro."

Connor, sunk in his misery, declined to say thanks. "See that third touchdown pass you threw. Real careless. If I had been shorter, that would have been an interception." Connor froze the tape at a point showing him leaping above an opponent to catch the ball higher in its arc.

"So we would have won 28-17. If it has to be football, can we just have a beer and watch the Monday night game?" Joe Dean settled in his chair.

"Fine with me." Connor stopped the recording and switched the screen to the game. "But don't touch my posters. In fact, don't even look at them."

****

Joe Dean was doing some light weight work the next day when one of the office staff came bearing a message. "Sorry to interrupt you, Joe, but I got a strange one on the phone."

"Another one of my honeys saying they'll commit suicide if I don't give up being celibate? Take the name and number and say I'll get back to them in the spring." Joe wiped the sweat off his hands.

"Nope. I think this is a guy. Someone named Jackie says there is an emergency situation concerning Stevie Dowd. I thought she was with Riley. Did you take his girl? Is that why Connor the Barbarian has a thorn in his ass this season?" the paper-pusher asked in a whisper because Riley worked out nearby. With his thinning hair and skinny body, Milt lived vicariously by taking messages to the players, as Joe knew very well.

"Hell, no! He'd never catch another pass for me again if I messed with Stevie, but I don't know about this Jackie guy. Bring me the phone."

A phone appeared immediately. Joe Dean wandered casually out of Connor's hearing range.

"This is Joe Dean Billodeaux. What's happening?"

"This is Jackie, Jackie Haile, the pro golfer," a low but not quite masculine voice said. "Stevie is traveling with the LPGA tour."

"Damn, I told Connor that Stevie might swing both ways," Joe burst out a little louder than he meant to. The wimp of a clerk who hovered nearby waiting to return the phone perked up, but Connor did not take notice.

"Get your mind out of the gutter, Billodeaux. I'm not having any luck that way, but Stevie is hurting really bad. She got drunk on Sunday so she wouldn't drive over to Atlanta and throw herself at Riley. Tell me he had an orgy after that game with six women. Tell me something I can use to help her get over him. She says you're one of his best friends. You ought to know something bad about him." The low voice got a little deeper.

"If I did, I wouldn't be telling you. Things aren't any better on this end. He plays a great game Sunday. Everyone's slapping him on the back, smacking his butt, and all he can say to me is 'Do you think Stevie was watching?' It's sickening. The guys are calling him Connor the Barbarian because he's always in a bad mood, real touchy, and it carries over on to the field. I can tell you there is more than one defensive player who is sorry he got in Riley's way this year. Even I get tired of being around him." Joe blew out a breath.

"I hate myself for suggesting it, but maybe we should try to get them back together. We're playing at The Woodlands this weekend. Stevie will be there," Jackie said.

"We have a bye-week. Maybe I can get over. Talk to her. Don't know what I can say, but it's worth a try. Let me put your number in my book. We'll think up something. Get back to you later."

Joe held out his hand for a pen from the waiting phone bearer and took down Jackie's cell number.

Now that was a good one, Jackie Haile's number in Joe Dean Billodeaux's little black book.

****

When Joe Dean Billodeaux, wearing a fitted black T-shirt and black jeans that showed off the well-developed muscles of his rear, walked on to the terrace at The Woodlands, conversation stopped. One of the amateur players, a girl barely out of high school, gaped at the epitome of tall, dark and handsome. He was well aware of the effect he had as he sauntered across the space.

Top golfer, Connie Parks, craned over her husband's bald spot and muttered, "Would you look at the devil who just walked in?"

Her good-natured man replied, "Honey, I'm sitting right here. That's not a devil. He's a Sinner. The New Orleans' quarterback. He was on TV last weekend when we were at Mount Vintage. Let me get an autograph to save for my girls. This guy is hot."

"I'll say," agreed Connie, her American girl freckled face pinking up a little.

Joe heard the brief conversation and the patter of Farley Parks' feet as the fan rushed over to pump his hand and offer a paper napkin and ballpoint pen.

"Say, Farley, that's F-A-R-L-E-Y, right? Could you tell me where Jackie Haile and Stevie Dowd might be hanging out?" He signed the napkin using the man's back as a writing surface.

"I think they went that a way. Jackie finished out of the money today same as my wife. She wasn't in a very sociable mood when we asked them to join us. But, come meet my wife, Connie Parks. You might have heard of her."

Joe took a moment to grasp Connie's hand. He looked into her pale blue eyes and said," A pleasure and a privilege, sugar."

The teen golfer seated two tables over gave out a warbling sigh. Joe flashed a smile her way, saw she was jail bait, and excused himself to go look for Jackie.

He found her sitting close to Stevie in a dim inside corner booth. The setup was perfect. He sure hoped this worked because he did not relish making an ass of himself for nothing. He strolled to their table and caught Jackie's quick wink in his direction.

"Well, well, Stevie Dowd. Long time no see," he greeted.

Stevie startled. "Joe, whatever are you doing here? How is Con—"

He cut her off. "Now I guess I know why you walked out on my best friend."

Jackie stood up and put a protective arm around Stevie. "She's with me, jerk. So let her alone. We're a couple now. Get lost."

"Jackie, no! Don't do this. We're only friends," Stevie sputtered.

"That's what they all say," Joe Dean insinuated.

"It's the truth!" Stevie frantically shrugged off Jackie's strong arm, but it descended to her waist and pulled her closer. "Don't tell Connor—"

"What, that you're a lesbian? Go back to New Orleans and tell him yourself if you want to give Connor a message. I'm out of here."

He oozed disgust and almost blew it by smiling. Maybe he could act someday when his football career was finished. He turned on his heel to leave, but Jackie, carrying the ploy one step further, grabbed his arm to spin him around. "You don't talk to my woman that way, you stupid jock bastard," Jackie snarled.

She was overacting, Joe Dean thought. Nerves. Probably explained her double bogey on the ninth hole and her failure to recover from it. He'd been watching the match and waiting to perform.

Joe straight-armed her into Stevie who fell back into the booth. Jackie swung at him and connected solidly with all the force of her fireplug body behind it.

"Hey, not my throwing arm, you dumb dyke," Joe shouted.

A camera flashed. Joe turned on the photographer, but the man hot-footed it toward the doors of the clubhouse.

Stevie struggled to her feet. "No, this isn't happening. You are both my friends." She clutched Joe's bruised arm and moved away from Jackie. "Stop it!"

"I'm telling Connor everything so he can stop crying in his beer over you, Stevie—unless you get to him first."

Joe Dean wanted to finish this and charge after the paparazzo. He knew where pictures like this ended up; he'd been on the cover of enough of those scandal sheets with various women and in occasional brawls, all of which he had given up this season. This is what trying to be a friend got you. He would probably be fined by the team if word got out.

"Tell Connor Riley she's mine," Jackie bellowed.

"I'll do that, bitch." Joe turned on his heel. Stevie trailed him. Maybe she would get in the car and come back to New Orleans with him for a happy reunion with Connor. No such luck. The paparazzo leaned out from behind a pillar and snapped Joe walking away from a pleading Stevie.

Jackie Haile tried to pull her back, asserting, "You're staying with me, baby doll."

"I can't, not if you act like this. I can't," Stevie wailed.

"Then get your things and come back to New Orleans with me," Joe told her.

"I can't. I can't bear it if he gets hurt again. I can't watch him play."

"Sure you can. It's his job. And right now, he's hurting on the inside more than the outside. Everyone's calling him Connor the Barbarian because he's such a grouch."

"Not Connor. He's always so kind, so laid back."

"Yes, Connor. The man you love?" Joe put it to the question.

He thought it made a nice touch. He forgot about the paparazzo until another flash went off. He whirled in that direction. This would not be the first camera he had smashed. The man backtracked hastily and sprinted through the swinging doors to the kitchen.

A waitress coming the other way with a tray held high fell to the floor as the photographer smashed into her. A salad course for six spewed into the air. Joe jumped over the server, slid on an avocado slice and landed on his side. By the time the quarterback scrambled up on the slippery footing of a bed of lettuce, the photographer had run through an exit and jumped into a waiting car.

Flicking avocado slime from his jeans, Joe returned to the women. "Sorry I couldn't catch him. Are you coming with me, Stevie?"

Jackie hung her head in great sorrow. "I guess I lost out to that big, blond Viking, huh? Alone again." She sighed and actually shed a tear. Joe would have been more impressed if he hadn't seen her pluck out a nose hair.

"Both of you leave me alone. Just leave me alone." In tears, Stevie ran from the building.

After she cleared the doors, Jackie looked at Joe. "Do you think we overplayed it?"

"We were great, too great, I think. But, if she shows up in New Orleans, it will be worth the trouble," Joe figured.

"I'll miss her. She was a friend, a really good friend. I don't have that many. You know a lot of the other girls on the tour are jealous of my abilities," Jackie confided.

"Yeah, I know how that is, *cher*. I know just how that is."

Chapter Eighteen

The scandal sheet came out just before the Sinners played the Panthers. The regular hype about the game on the sports pages went on and on about both quarterbacks being from the Louisiana bayous, Chapelle being only forty miles from Carencro. How Joe and Johnny Delacroix had played against each other in the parochial league, though Joe was a little younger. The media dubbed it *The Battle of the Deux Cajuns - Bad Boy Versus Altar Boy*. Joe reveled in the notoriety. Good stuff for selling tickets. The Super Dome sold out, and every sports bar between New Orleans and Alexandria packed full to overflowing.

The general management shrugged off the full color spread of Joe's escapade at The Woodlands in the less than merciful tabloid. Just more free publicity for the game garnered by their trouble prone quarterback. However, Coach Buck personally took a piece out of Joe Dean Billodeaux. The team mumbled about a fine when they saw the bruise on Joe's throwing arm and the stiff way he turned to the side. Connor Riley would not talk to him at all.

The banner on the tabloid screamed *Sinners' Quarterback fights Lesbian Golfer for Best Friend's Lover*. The chosen picture showed Jackie Haile punching Joe in his throwing arm while Stevie looked on tearfully. Inside the cover, another shot portrayed Stevie supposedly imploring Joe Dean to "make me not a lesbian." While personally Joe had confidence he could convert any lesbian back into heterosexuality, Connor had not taken the article well.

"What the fuck were you doing in Texas with Stevie?" Riley asked tersely when Joe finally prodded him into speech.

"Trying to bring her home to you, asshole. And look what it got me—a bad arm, a possible fine, who knows what other misery."

"I told you to let him grieve, Joe," the Rev intervened. "These two will either come together their own selves or get over it."

"We were pretending it was an intervention. You know, me saving her from Jackie's clutches. Then Stevie, she was supposed to run home to you. I guess she didn't, did she?" Joe asked hopefully.

"I don't know where she is now. Before, I could record golf matches and sometimes see her in the background, know she was okay. Now I don't know where she is. Thanks a bunch for screwing with my life." Connor stalked away. He had not said a word to his quarterback since.

The game did not go any better. The first half turned into a defensive slug fest with no score but enough close calls to keep the crowd riveted to the seats. At halftime instead of enjoying the performance of the flashy Southern band, the fans waited in lines a half a mile long for the restrooms.

Second half, Joe couldn't make it out of the pocket, and he was sacked twice by a particularly aggressive nose tackle. He completed a few short passes to his running back, but none that even got them into field goal range. He swore to Coach Buck the bruise on his arm had nothing to do with it, but Coach did not cut him any slack. Finally, they agreed if Joe could shake free, he might try a few long passes to Riley. Connor nodded to show he had heard the plan.

Near the end of the still scoreless third quarter, Joe broke free, took aim and fired a long pass to Riley. Connor was there to receive, but being nickeled and dimed by the Panthers' defense. The ball barely fell into his grasp before he hit the ground hard. The pigskin bounced free across the artificial turf. Connor was on it, covering the fumble with his big body, but the two backs pressuring him piled on top hoping to squeeze the ball out from under him. Riley's helmet popped off.

Whistles blew. The opposing players rose from the heap and left Riley in possession of the ball. Red-faced, Connor got up and shoved one of the backs into the other. He took a swing at the man. His opponent dodged. Joe grabbed his receiver's arm trying to prevent more damage. Connor threw him off and went after his opponent again. The whistles blew and blew. Riley got in the official's face and was thrown out of the game. Angry and unrepentant, Connor Riley took his place on the bench with Coach Buck chewing on his ear.

On the next play, Joe turned over the ball on a pass to Deets. The Panthers scored on that fatal mistake. Delacroix connected with one long pass in the fourth quarter. The final score came in at 0-14, the Panthers. The Sinners took their first loss of the season.

With Connor crashing, Joe Dean sat in the locker room and envisioned all his sacrifices—his irksome celibacy, his pretty good behavior, his trying to do the right thing—going right down the toilet along with a chance at another Super Bowl.

He wanted to be a strong team leader but didn't know if he had it in him. The Rev kept saying just to be Connor's friend, be there for him. Hell, he should let the Rev be the team captain. But, the Rev said no, that was Joe's job. He needed to learn it and learn it well. Never strong on academics, what did he know about depression and psychology? Joe Dean Billodeaux was an expert in only two things, sex and football, and neither were going to help Connor Riley.

Chapter Nineteen

In Houston, Stevie Dowd's brother-in-law watched the game. Stevie had taken her nieces to the Space Center where they wore themselves out playing astronaut and fell asleep in the Imax. She brought them home a little earlier than intended. Brent, his soft, past-thirty body stretched out in a plaid recliner, a bottle of beer in his hand and bag of pork rinds nearby, called out to her as she passed by his lair.

"You've got to see this, Stevie. Your old lover boy got thrown out of the game. With a temper like that no wonder you left him."

She could not resist scratching the itch to see Connor. He was muscling through the after-game crowd on the field pursued by a reporter. "Give us your side, Connor."

"No comment," he replied and continued moving toward the locker room.

The Rev filled the screen as if he were blocking for his friend. "Give the man his space. It was a hard fought battle against a top team. We lost, and we apologize to the hometown fans who came here to see this game. But it's our first loss, and we still going all the way to the top. You hear me!"

The scene flashed back to the press box where the commentators, Al and Hank,interviewed a noted sports psychologist. "Doctor, how do you account for the change in personality of Connor Riley, once known as one of the most easygoing players in the game, now called Connor the Barbarian by his own team?"

"A serious, life-threatening injury such as Mr. Riley suffered at the end of the last season can bring about such a change in personality. When his helmet came off, surely he remembered that awful moment in Seattle. He was not striking out against these players, but against the one who nearly destroyed him in the past. With time, his anger and fear might fade. If he cannot control these emotions, his career will end as certainly as it would have with a major injury," the psychologist intoned sagely. The film of Connor on the bottom of the pile, the helmet coming off and the ensuing fight played as the doctor spoke.

"Oh, God, no." Stevie, shaky, watched the replay, hardly hearing the voice of the psychologist.

Her sister Michelle, short, plump, and maternal, so like their mother, passed by taking two cranky little girls upstairs for naps. "Get over it, Stevie. You ditched Connor Riley, and it looks like a good thing you did. Let it go. You're getting on everyone's nerves. Even Mom is avoiding you."

"Home," thought Stevie, remembering a favorite bit of poetry, "is the place where, when you have go there, they have to take you in" —Robert Frost, a death poem.

She'd coped so far by flying out on weekends to keep her obligations with *Golf*. At least, Houston was a hub with decent airfares available to almost anywhere. At the tournaments, she avoided being with Jackie outside of offering a cordial hello. As soon as the event ended, she got back on a plane to Houston.

One downside of passing through the airport so frequently—on Sundays, the bars and restaurants and sitting areas turned their television sets on to the Sinners' games. The team sat at the top of their division, but their white-hot season start was steadily cooling off. They won on field goals, blocked extra points, and two point conversions now. Last week, they lost a second game.

She arrested her progress through the terminal again and again stopping to stare at Connor Riley. Each week, he seemed to deteriorate further. Any time he got tackled, he rose up ready to fight, shouting to the ref that he had been fouled. Replays showed this was rarely the case. On one occasion, she caught a sports montage entitled *Connor the Barbarian's Tackle Tantrums.* A background chorus of boos came from fans on both sides.

Riley spent more and more time on the bench. His golden hair hung lank half hiding his gaunt, unshaven face. Stevie wished she could push the hair back and wash it slowly with her fingertips as she had often done when they showered together, her body slick against his. His eyes stayed cast down towards the space between his cleated shoes. He appeared divorced from the game and everyone around him.

As Stevie knew because Connor feared being replaced while he lay in a bed in Seattle, the Sinners management had brought up a new first year player named Jared Forte for training when they were in doubt if Riley would play again. Their new wide receiver was fast as a blue runner snake but lacked Connor's strength to shake off defenders and his uncanny ability to be where Joe Dean Billodeaux needed him. Still, young Jared got more and more playing time and improved with the experience.

The sports show commentators conjectured Connor Riley would be released at the end of this season, a sad end to a once brilliant career. The history of football was filled with such stories. Stevie tried to keep herself from remembering how much Connor had suffered, how hard he had tried to come back, only to end his playing days this way. If he had just listened to her...no, she would not go there again.

She made it through Thanksgiving with her family, the meal an agonizing ordeal. Her balding brother-in-law could not keep quiet about what an asshole Connor Riley was. Her mother, fluffy-haired and dressed in ruffles, but as sharp-tongued and critical as ever when it came to her younger daughter, commented that if Stevie had married the man last spring, she would have had grounds for divorce now, gotten an nice pile of alimony, and never have had to work another day in her life.

Usually sweet Michelle grew outraged by the suggestion her sister should have married that brute for his money. Who knew what he might have done to her? The guy was probably psychotic on steroids.

Little Betsy asked what psychotic steroids were. "Bad, bad drugs, lamb," her mommy told her. Stevie took her unfinished meal back to the kitchen, went upstairs and packed her bags.

She stayed on the road for three weeks ending up in Las Vegas for the last tournament of the golf tour. Like the Sinners, Jackie Haile's season had started out sweet, then soured. Still, she would clear over $500,000 this year once she added in her third place prize money for this day's work. Despite trying to avoid the golfer, Stevie found herself cornered by Jackie and asked her out for a celebration dinner, no strings attached. Stevie looked like she needed a good feeding, Jackie claimed. That was all there was to it—that and so much more.

"You know, baby doll, dumb as our little act for your benefit was, Joe Dean and I have stayed in touch. No fooling. We talk all the time, me and that jock," Jackie confessed. "He says I keep his mind off of women, can you believe that?"

"Sounds like something Joe would say," Stevie answered sawing off a piece of rare prime rib with a serrated steak knife big enough to be a lethal weapon. She'd tried to order a grilled chicken sandwich, but Jackie insisted she was too pale and needed red meat for the iron. She saw no easy escape from a long meal in Jackie's company.

"Oh, he's not so bad. You know, once I told him that after I came out, I was no longer welcome in my parents' house. They're kind of religious and all. He remembered that, and last time we talked, he asked if I had a place to spend Christmas. At his mama's house there's always room for one more at the table. I said, 'Why Joe Dean, aren't you afraid I'll corrupt your many nieces', and he says, 'Nah, they're all feisty girls who can either take you or outrun you.' Still, I was touched."

"But do you have a place to go? I wish I could issue an invitation, but my mother would feel she had to lock up her granddaughters for the day," Stevie explained.

"Hey, I have an older sister, married with three boys. We were always close. She used to keep the other kids from teasing me because I wanted to wear boy's clothes. Not that I couldn't punch them out for myself, but it's nice to have someone on your side. Good old Paulette. I'm leaving everything I have to her sons since I'm not likely to have any of my own. There is much to be said for having someone love and accept you just the way you are. That's pretty rare."

Jackie paused to take a sip of her red wine. Stevie ate and listened.

"You know, my dad taught me golf. For years, I was the son he never had. I got a golf scholarship to college and he was so proud. Then, I brought Darlene home and told my parents this was my girlfriend. They said they were always happy to meet my friends. I said, no, Darlene and I were in love. Dad told us to leave his house. I pleaded with him to love me as I am. I was sorry, but I couldn't change for him. Please, just to keep on loving me."

Stevie choked on a dry piece of roll. At least, she pretended that. She hid her face behind her water glass, swallowed and said, "You still had Darlene."

"For a while. I graduated, went on the tour. She

wanted to settle down in San Francisco. I was gone a lot. When I came home, she had someone else. Old story. Joe has heard it. Mostly though, we just joke around. He says he needs some comic relief since sitting with Connor is like spending the night in a hospice full of dying people. Sorry, I didn't mean to mention that name at my celebration dinner," Jackie apologized.

"So you talk about us," Stevie accused.

"Not really. The first time Joe called you Steel-hearted Stevie I said you were off-limits. I did not want to hear about Connor Riley's breakdown." Jackie savagely stabbed her baked potato with a fork and pulled out a steaming, white chunk dripping with butter.

"Breakdown?" Stevie's voice quivered. "Is this another one of your ploys to get me to go back to New Orleans?"

"Hell, no. Maybe it isn't a breakdown. Joe just said they made Connor go see the team shrink. He goes, but isn't cooperating. Tells the guy he doesn't want to be touched, and that's it. Of course, if I had been through what he has, I might feel the same way, but it's not my problem. Let the shrink straighten him out. I never met the man. Would you like to order the cherries jubilee for dessert? I love to watch them serve it with all those blue flames licking the ice cream. Or chocolate mousse, isn't that one of your favorites?" Jackie continued to eat while Stevie carefully set down her knife and fork and blotted her mouth with the linen napkin.

"I appreciate the meal, Jackie, but I want to get to the airport early, so I'll skip dessert. Thanks." Stevie rose to leave.

"Any time, baby doll. I'm glad we're friends again. Where should I send your Christmas card? I don't think I have your Houston address." Jackie pulled out a BlackBerry and prepared to enter a new address.

"I'll be in New Orleans at my old place. Stop by if you get to town." Stevie needed, wanted to leave.

"A hug then, for old times sake."

Jackie gave her a squeeze and sent Stevie on her way in a hurry.

The pro golfer ordered the cherries jubilee for her dessert and had the waiter bring her a good cigar to enjoy on the walk back to her hotel. Not easy to find a quiet spot in Vegas, so she waited to call until she was back in her suite.

"Hey, sex maniac," Jackie greeted.

"How's it hanging, bull dyke?" Joe Dean answered.

"Lower than yours, I'd bet. What are you doing right now?"

"I just got out of the shower, and I'm wearing nothing but a towel slung low on my very fine hips. Am I getting to you?" Joe said with a leer in his voice.

"Yeah, you're turning me off. I missed the end of the game because I had dinner with an old friend. How did the Sinners make out?"

"Best game in weeks. Forte finally got under one of my passes, and Deets caught a long one, too. The Rev did his magic, and Ancient Andy was right on the mark. We have the division championship wrapped up. We can sit back and rest while the wild cards duke it out this year."

"Congratulations. I came in a close third this time myself, but still, a $500,000 year is nothing to spit on. Maybe I can afford a Super Bowl ticket," she hinted.

"I'll send you one if you promise not to bring a date. Since I'm making fifteen million a year now, I can afford to be generous," Joe boasted.

"That's obscene—another example of the inequity between men's and women's sports. I can buy my own ticket since I'm not one of your bimbos."

"Yeah, yeah. Heard it all before."

"But you don't listen. I said I had dinner with an old friend. An old friend named Stevie Dowd."

"Steel-hearted Stevie? I hope she's miserable. I'm on my way to Connor's right now. He had a bad day glued to the bench. This was a crucial game and Coach thought he'd cost us yardage in penalties. I guess he would have put him in if Deets and Forte hadn't come through, but they did. I should be out celebrating, but the temptations are less over at the Riley hospice for the lovelorn. I'm on my way over there. You know, with no women around, I have to get my own beer."

"Wish I were lovelorn. Stevie must have dropped twenty pounds, and I could stand to lose some myself. Say, I thought you were just coming out of the shower?" Jackie countered.

"Toying with you, sugar," Joe Dean teased.

"Anyhow, I was about to tell you she cracked. She's on her way to New Orleans. I hope that story you told me about the shrink is true because I don't want her mad at me again."

"God's honest truth. I hate that shrink. They sent me to him once to discuss my, quote, sexual addiction. I still say there is nothing wrong with loving women, lots of women."

"I agree with you there, bro," Jackie chimed in.

"Always good to be backed up by a lesbian. Anyhow, he tried to tell me my insecurity about my abilities as a quarterback caused me to overcompensate by scoring with women. I never went back. I saw the guy again while I waited for Connor. Four months, I told him, four months without women. He said he applauded my reaching a new level of maturity. I bet he never gets any."

"If you can get your mind off yourself, you might mention Stevie is back in town and give your friend a little lift. As for me, I sure as hell hope my dad never finds out I told her he kicked me out for being a lesbian. He would be so pissed. Dad is my biggest fan. And then there was the Darlene story."

"Who's Darlene?" Joe Dean had to ask.

"My supposed college lover who could not accept my career choice. Remember that detail, please. Also, you invited me for Christmas in Chapelle."

"But of course I did. My mama would feed you up, and my male cousins would try to straighten you out. You are welcome anytime," Joe offered.

"God help me if there are more like you back on the bayou."

"*Beaucoup*, Jacqueline, but they cannot throw zee football," he joked, putting on his best French accent.

"That's all I can take tonight. I'll be at my sister's place for Christmas as usual. Keep me posted, jackass."

"*Bonsoir*, bull dyke."

Oh that Jackie, she did make him laugh, and he needed some laughs right now. Joe Dean pushed his speedometer up to eighty, no big deal in Louisiana and after today's game if he were stopped, there would be no ticket; only a few autographs handed out. He felt a need for speed.

Connor had ducked out as usual while most of the guys were in the showers. No need to shower when you didn't play, but the man didn't shave or fix up to go out for a victory celebration either. Once, he caught the former best wide receiver in the league sitting on the locker room bench rocking back and forth like one of those monkey babies deprived of its mother or in this case, Stevie Dowd. Connor stopped as soon as Joe noticed. Stevie sure had wrecked a great player. Now she was coming back, just in time maybe, and Joe got to deliver the great news. He would do anything for his team. Didn't his celibacy vow show that?

Crossing the long concrete bridge spanning Lake

Ponchartrain, Joe kept his eye out for accidents. A foot on the accelerator and Connor's nice little Jag could top those guardrails easy. Yes, things had gotten that bad, and he was scared as hell about what he would find at Riley's house.

Connor's gate stood open again, and his door was unlocked—damned careless considering how rabid fans could be. He was none too popular right now. It took only one lunatic who thought he was doing the team a favor by taking out Connor Riley to barge in with a gun. Welcome to my home. Come on in and shoot me. Maybe that's what Connor wanted.

The house, dark and quiet, not even a game tape playing, gave Joe Dean a chill up his back. The only lights shone on Stevie's pictures in the den. Connor sat slumped in his leather recliner. For a moment Joe thought his friend was dead from an overdose, but the broad chest did move slowly up and down. His eyes were open, but he said nothing. Was this a mental breakdown in progress? How the hell would a quarterback know?

"How's it going, Connor?"

"A thing of beauty is a joy forever," Connor quoted, staring at Stevie's pinups.

"Something we read in high school? Some poem about big jugs, right?" Joe guessed.

"Keats. *Ode to a Grecian Urn*. Stevie said that about her sports photography. She said the pictures she took of me were things of beauty. Good she can't see me now, huh? They didn't need me in the game. I never left the bench."

"Whose fault is that? You got to snap out of it, man. Never mind. I have some news you need to hear," Joe rushed on.

"They aren't going to renew my contract, are they?"

"I have no idea. Stevie is back in town."

"It's too late, Joe, too late. Why don't you take those posters down and carry them home with you.

Don't throw them out, though. They are things of beauty." Connor closed his eyes as if waiting to hear the sound of paper being torn off the wall but not wanting to watch.

"Let's leave them be, bro. I plan to spend the night."

Joe Dean stretched out in the other recliner. He picked up the remote and channel surfed. Connor took no interest at all. Finally, he came across a John Wayne film festival. Just what the doctor ordered. *The Sands of Iwo Jima, The Alamo, The Horse Soldiers, She Wore a Yellow Ribbon,* all were movies about brave stands and great victories, even that last one with the sissy title. John Wayne never gave up and probably didn't know the meaning of the word "depression".

Joe thought about getting a beer, but no. Alcohol would make matters worse. If he got Connor through the night, he could call in reinforcements come morning. And the Rev better get the fuck over here sooner than those slackers who were supposed to relieve the Alamo.

Chapter Twenty

Joe Dean Billodeaux woke to the smell of dark roast coffee wafting through the house. Stiff, he crawled out of the recliner and did a few quick stretches. In the other chair, Connor slept on, his head skewed to one side. Joe was damned grateful the man had not gotten up in the night. How uncomfortable to follow a friend to the bathroom filled as it was with things like pills and razor blades and not give some kind of explanation. Quietly in stocking feet, he left the den and headed for the kitchen.

Eula Mae and Miss Essie were enjoying a cup of Community brew and sharing a copy of the *Times Picayune.* Joe saw Eula Mae cover a tabloid that had his picture on the front with one of her big hands. He pretended not to see and began issuing orders.

"In an hour or so, we'll want breakfast—grits, eggs, bacon, whole wheat toast, orange juice and coffee."

Little gray-haired Miss Essie continued to sip her dark roast blend. "Mr. Connor says he don't want nothing but coffee no more. I already been told three times I'm not his mama, and I don't want to lose my job."

"Speaking of which, where is Mrs. Riley? I don't think she's the kind to stand by and do nothing when her son is in trouble. She spent months in Seattle watching over him," Joe Dean asked.

"Mr. Connor sent his folks on their dream cruise right after Thanksgiving. Gonna see England, Scotland, Wales and Ireland, then come home for

Christmas. A early present, he says. Gettin' them out the way, I says. His brother got the company to run and all them kids, so he's not around neither," Eula Mae answered.

"Phone." Joe Dean held out his hand.

Eula Mae gave him an 'I don't work for you' look and pointed. "Right there by you."

Joe dialed the phone on the counter and woke up the Rev. "You tear your big black ass away from Mintay and your wedding plans and get down to Connor's place. I need some help. You're the one wants to be a preacher some day. You can get some practice in right now. Good. I'm counting on you."

Connor, apparently following the smell of the coffee, straggled into the kitchen. He seemed bleary-eyed and sluggish even though they had done no drinking the night before, only watched old war movies far into the night.

"Skip the coffee and put on your running shoes. I figure we can run a few miles before breakfast," Joe announced.

"What if I don't want to run?" Connor groused.

"Then I'll be assuming it's because you let yourself get in such sad shape that I am now faster than you, super star," Joe challenged.

"You're wrong."

"Prove it. We got an hour or so while these fine ladies get breakfast to cooking." Joe moved down the hallway to find the upper end Nikes he had shucked off in the den the night before. Connor followed reluctantly.

They stretched on the portico, then slowly jogged down the long drive to the open gate. Turning along the lakeshore road, Joe picked up the pace gradually until he figured they had reached a good halfway point. He turned and appealed to Connor's competitive nature.

"I figure I can beat you back to the house with no trouble at all, big deal wide receiver."

Connor took off with Joe on his heels. By the time they were half way back to the house, Connor had gotten far enough out in front to run backwards and taunt, "Who's in lousy shape, smart-ass quarterback?"

He waited by the gate until Joe caught up. Both men were sweating but not winded. They cooled down on the long driveway.

Breakfast waited on the table when they got in. "Looks great, Miss Essie. Feel like eating now, Connor?"

"Yeah. I guess I could eat." He did, abundantly for the first time in weeks.

"Okay, now," Joe Dean instructed. "Go get cleaned up, and I mean showered, shaved, and that girly hair washed. We got a team meeting, and I know you have an appointment with Dr. Mind Fuck at eleven. Don't deny it. You spill that sack of shit you been carrying around all over him. After that, we drive down Poydras, cut over to the French Market. You buy a bouquet of freakin' daisies while I circle the block so we don't have to waste time trying to park. I pick you up in front of the Central Grocery. I know Stevie is back in town, hence the daisies. Need I say more? We do a diagonal to her place, and you go in to score. I'll wait in the car for as long as it takes."

"She won't be there," Connor insisted. "Stevie is gone forever."

"I'm the quarterback. I call the plays," Joe Dean asserted.

****

Things went pretty much as Joe Dean Billodeaux called them. When Connor left the doctor whose actual name was Edwin Funk, the psychiatrist said a few parting words at the door. "Good progress today, Mr. Riley. A breakthrough."

Joe Dean tossed down the *Golf* magazine he had been passing the time with and said, "Hey, Doc, four sexless months."

"I commend you, too, Mr. Billodeaux. Excellent progress, both of you." Dr. Funk shut his door with a crisp snap.

"That man is going to be so disappointed come February. I figure if I do two a day, I won't run out of women until training camp starts. I've been thinking of going semi-celibate next year, cutting back on cunt while I'm playing. Seems to help my game."

"Joe Dean, you are either celibate or you aren't. There is no such thing as being semi-celibate," Connor corrected him.

"Well, there should be, I mean as rewards for good behavior. Yes, indeed."

Joe did the driving and managed to circle the block in the sluggish New Orleans traffic without hitting any tourists or getting scratches on his little red sports car. By the time he got back, Connor had the daisies and two giant muffuletta sandwiches stuffed with cold cuts and olive salad and wrapped in waxed paper to go.

"Feeling better? Hungry?"

"I guess so," Connor admitted as he slid into the car while horns blared behind them.

They raced to Stevie's place. Daisies in hand, Connor took the steps up to her door two at a time. No one answered his knock. He came back down, looked around the back and returned to where Joe Dean waited.

"She's not here. I told you so," he said glumly.

"Maybe she went for groceries. Remember how little stuff she had in the refrigerator when we brought her home from the hospital?" Joe relied on the memory to lighten the situation.

Connor did smile slightly. "I don't think Stevie is much of a cook. She probably picked up her car and headed out of town again. Her coming home had nothing to do with me." He slouched into the shotgun seat of the low-slung, red Porsche.

"Hey, watch the sandwiches. I don't want olive juice all over my leather upholstery. We'll try again later after lunch and a light workout."

"Yeah, sure." Connor remained surly all the way across the lake causeway.

****

Stevie Dowd headed out of town. She crossed the causeway and drove through the piney woods to the cypress-studded lakeshore where the rich and sometimes famous lived. She had dredged the key to Connor's house from the desk drawer where she'd thrown it before joining the LPGA tour. She'd meant to mail it back to him. At least, she thought she had, but she never did. Here the key lay in her hand, ready to use again if she could work up the courage.

She'd always regarded Jackie as an amusing friend, not particularly deep, same as Joe Dean, until that dinner in Las Vegas. Jackie had been hurt by her Darlene but moved on to have a great career. Maybe Connor had moved on, too. No, she knew his career was tanking. Worst of all, Stevie knew she was his Darlene, a person who had dumped him because of her own fears and desires. Connor might not want her back.

She would admit to being wrong about not supporting his dream to play again. She would stay with him no matter what. He didn't have to say he loved her or repeat his proposal. This time Stevie Dowd would stick to a relationship and make it work...if she got a second chance. And, she would not try anything underhanded like pulling a Merrilee and getting pregnant to keep him. She needed to talk with Connor long and hard and now.

The gate to the house was sealed tight of course. No telling if Connor was home. She cringed at using the call box. Disgusted with the way her hands sweat and her heart pumped faster, she sat in her idling car like some kind of groupie waiting for her hero to appear. She should have called first to see if she was welcome. Courage draining, Stevie backed up her car, swung it around, and prepared to return to New Orleans.

Once she got across the lake, she'd call instead of lurking outside his gate like a stalker. If he hung up, she'd try again—the way Connor had over and over. Remorse engulfed her like water from a broken levee. Stevie put her foot on the brake and covered her face with her hands to hold in the tears. A red Porsche tearing down the center of the road as if it were pursuing her in a high-speed chase nearly hit her car. Joe Dean braked his expensive ride diagonally across the road.

"Get out and don't come back until—what's the word—you two have a breakthrough," Joe ordered his passenger, but Connor was already in the street approaching Stevie.

She felt as nervous and guilty as a criminal and Joe Dean probably thought of her that way. She'd committed a crime against his team, his friend.

Connor opened her door, drew Stevie to him, and kissed her so hard her back bent across the hood. He waved to Joe for a little privacy.

Joe Dean flipped down his sun visor. He slumped into a "they're going to be awhile position", unwrapped a muffuletta, took a bite from a wedge and sucked the olive oil off his fingers. Coming out of the clutch, Stevie stared his way. He gave her a friendly salute with his sandwich as Connor led her home. That jerk, always around when she needed to be alone with the man she loved.

Connor opened the gate and the couple walked slowly down drive, around the house, and across the deck to the dock. They did not say a word as they watched the light chop of the water, the boats swaying, a blue heron passing on the wing. Neither seemed able to speak.

Finally heeding Joe Dean's orders, Connor began. "Stevie, I haven't been playing fair. I treated you like some bonus I deserved because I had a great season and did the celibacy thing last year. I wasn't honest with you. I used you cover up my real problem."

She closed her eyes against the glare on the water and kept them closed. It was going to happen again. This man was going to hurt her more deeply than any of the others because she loved him heart and soul.

Sure, she'd thought maybe Kevin was the one when she'd been young and stupid. Close call there. Then, she'd rebounded with the slick Marcello. How surprised had she been when Marcello left with his completed portfolio before she finished her studies in Italy? Not much. As for Dex, he turned out to be more of a convenient business and sexual partner than anything else. Her fury at his duplicity had driven Dex out of her mind completely. But this one, this one would to destroy her.

"I'm afraid when I play, afraid of another injury. I covered it up well early in the season when we were playing weak teams and no one could catch me. When I recovered that fumble, they piled on top of me. My helmet was torn off. I thought for a moment I couldn't feel my toes. Anger, I used anger so no one would know how scared I was. Worse, I let everyone think you were to blame for my temper, my slump."

Connor stared into the water of the lake sloshing beneath his shoes, not looking at Stevie. His long hair fell across his cheeks shielding him from her gaze.

His pose was so like the one she had witnessed when he sat on the bench during the last game that Stevie reached out and pushed back his hair as she had been longing to do for months. The golden strands were clean now but needed a trim badly. Her fingers smoothed the blond locks behind his ears and followed the strands down his neck, lightly touching the scars from his surgery until they came to rest warmly on his shoulders. He shivered beneath her hands.

"You could have told me. I would have understood."

"And said what?"

"Quit playing."

"Right. If I quit, then I was admitting I was afraid. You have to play strong if you are going to play the game. I let you go rather than confess the real problem."

"I should have known. I should have stayed." She hated herself for not seeing this. She was even more ashamed for thinking of herself as the sole reason for Connor's problems, so certain of his love that when she looked into his eyes, she saw only her reflection and nothing more.

"You would have stayed with me if I was paralyzed, right?"

"Yes, you couldn't drive me away."

"But I tried to because I wasn't the man you fell in love with. I'm still not."

"I'll stay with you now if you want me to. If it's not too late for us."

"Last night, I thought so. Coach benched me last game, and I was relieved I didn't have to play. I thought my career had ended. No one would ever know how scared I was because they could only see the anger I used to cover up."

"If you came back to me, you might see what the others had missed—that I wasn't the big, brave jock anymore, but an impostor. You were better gone. My career is over. I should have been home free with no one the wiser. Then it hit me: I had nothing worth living for. I passed the worst night of my life yesterday. Joe stayed by me. Today, I told Dr. Funk what was eating me. I'm doing a little better."

"Joe is a good friend…a jerk, but a good friend." Stevie wiped a tear, pretending the wind troubled her eyes. "The stunt he pulled to get me back here even when he blamed me for your condition you wouldn't believe. Sure, it ran in the tabloids, but you had to be there. Jackie did her best, too. She finally made me see I had to stand by you, no matter what—that is if you still want me."

"I need to finish the season or the fear will win. Can you bear it?"

"I will for as long as you need me. Can't they give you any extra protection? Can't the trainers do anything for you?"

"They tried at the beginning of the season. I had a neck guard, but it was uncomfortable. I couldn't turn my head the way I wanted. Besides, I considered it a sissy thing. Made me look weak, so I refused to wear it because I'm big, tough Connor Riley." He gave Stevie a sad smile.

"Could you try it again? Work with it until it's comfortable?"

"Yeah. I'll do that."

"And Connor, I think I'd like to talk to Dr. Funk myself if you could arrange it."

"We'll go together."

"I can think of another place we can go together. Right now. If the back door is open."

"You have the key, Stevie."

****

Eula Mae, her big arms filled with sheets, padded down the hall toward Mr. Connor's suite. For the first time in a month she had beard stubble to clean out of the sink and long blond hair to pluck from the shower drain. She pulled up when she saw the bedroom door closed. The breathing and moaning going on in there was so heavy she could hear it through the cracks. She did a U-turn and headed back toward the kitchen where she tossed the sheets on a counter and poured herself an iced tea from the pitcher her mother set on kitchen table along with a light lunch of chicken salad sandwiches and cantaloupe slices.

"Mama, Mr. Connor got someone in his bedroom."

"Way things is going around here, let's hope it ain't Mr. Joe."

"Mama! I was thinking they found Miss Stevie."

"It's them trashy tabloids you always reading, child, that puts ideas into my head. Miss Stevie would be good. I liked her. She stayed out of my kitchen and never complained about the food. But could be Mr. Joe ordered him to pick up a woman downtown if she wasn't around. He was mighty bossy this morning. Seemed to know just what Mr. Connor needed."

"Amen," answered Eula Mae, settling her large behind into a seat and getting ready for an early lunch before she tackled the bathroom.

****

Stevie was half way through a full body kiss when she heard footsteps in the hall. She'd started with Connor's forehead, brushed her lips down his hollowed cheeks, lingered on his full lips, inhaled the scent of aftershave on his clean-shaven chin. She slid down his neck into the golden chest hair, tongued each of his nipples and continued on down his torso, skirting an erection so hard and purposeful it tilted in her direction when she began kissing the inside of his thigh. Every scar, every bruise, received extra attention from her lips. She was making her way up Connor's left calf muscle, hard as quick-set concrete, when she heard the sounds and paused.

Connor let out a groan that seemed to shake the bedroom door. He raised her up and set her on the erection that had followed her pathway toward the other side of his body like a sexual magnet. Stevie heaved an enormous sigh. He turned them over accompanied by a symphony of bedspring squeaks. The footsteps in the hall receded.

Stevie expected the sex to go quickly, not that it mattered a bit. She had aroused herself paying court to every inch of his body and she was ready, but Connor took his time. He circled her ears with his tongue, lingered on her lips, plundered her mouth, then moved down the long sweep of her neck to the adoration of her breasts, one at a time, sucking each pink nipple until Stevie began the restless motion herself. She crossed her long legs at the top of his thighs and pushed hard. Smiling, Connor picked up the rhythm of love and mighty good sex.

****

Joe Dean got cramped in the Porsche. How long did it take to say 'I love you' and jump in the sack? He had no idea, never having said those three words to any of his women. He was mopping the olive juice from the leather seat with a paper napkin when the Rev pulled up in his Escalade.

"What's going down, bro? I been looking for you since team meeting. Want me to spend the night here?"

"About time you showed up. Mintay let you off the leash? You don't have to rush back to Chapelle and pick out china patterns or something?" Joe growled.

"She's a doctor, Joe Dean. She's cool with it. If Connor needs me here, I'm here. Say, that a muffuletta from Central Grocery? I missed my feed searching for y'all."

The Rev's brawny, brown arm shot out to snag the second sandwich off the front seat. He pulled the paper back from the bread and took a big mouthful. "Best in town," he said, his lips shiny with oil. "So where's Connor. Shouldn't we be with him?"

"If we're lucky, Stevie will be spending the night. She's in there right now restoring Connor's confidence. Tonight, you and me can go some place restful—like a jazz club."

"Fine by me, but no titty bars. Mintay would smell it on me and cancel the nuptials in a flash. So, Stevie Dowd is back. Guess I'm glad—though that woman sure was a disappointment, abandoning Connor in his time of need."

"Look, it took Jackie and me months to get her back here. Don't fuck it up by getting in her face the next time you see her. I got everything fixed up fine now between Stevie and Connor."

The Rev raised a skeptical eyebrow. "I think it's gonna take more than an afternoon of sex to repair this mess. They got issues to discuss. Might need a long time to sort things out."

"If they need more help, I can sic St. Jude on 'em. He sure came through for me. I stay celibate for the season. Connor gets well and plays again. Maybe I can work another deal for them."

"Joe Dean, you got the simple faith of a child. The Bible says that's a good thang, but you know, folks have to work on their problems, too."

"I don't see why when a prayer and a nice donation to the Catholic Church will take care of the matter."

"Okay, you the man. You call the plays," the Rev said around a mouthful of ham, cheese, and salami. "Who am I to say miracles don't happen?"

"Damn right. I am the quarterback. Yes, I am."

"So, Mr. Quarterback, you think we could move these cars before a neighbor thinks this is a three-car accident and calls the police. You know I'd be the one they arrest. After that, I could use some cold sweet tea or a beer to wash down this sandwich. Figure we could sneak in the kitchen door without upsetting whatever is going on in the bedroom?"

"Good plan, Rev. Let's go with it."

Chapter Twenty-One

The rest of the Sinners thundered through the tunnel to the field, but Coach Buck put a restraining hand on Connor Riley's shoulder. "A moment, son."

Connor stopped dead and lowered his head. Just when things were coming together for him, Coach was going to rip him apart. He deserved it of course. The man had put up with too much crap; grounded him last week, and now would deliver a final blow, probably giving Forte his place in the lineup permanently.

"How's that neck guard working out for you?"

"Good, Coach, real good. They lowered the sides so I can turn my head better, put in a little more padding to make it comfortable. It works for me."

"Glad to hear it. I also hear Stevie Dowd is back in your life. Women... Women can be more treacherous than football." Coach Buck nodded, agreeing with himself from long experience. "I have two ex-wives and a cold bed to prove it."

"Me and Stevie, we're good." Connor's blazing smile made the coach smile back, deepening the lines around his mouth and eyes.

"Glad to hear it. About today."

Connor braced for bad news and began arranging his arguments about why he should play in this game.

"Doc Funk says I should play you, but I want your word, no outbursts, no tantrums that will cost the team. Early in the season, you ran rings around these jokers and they may be out to get you, so be aware."

Connor nodded. Coach raked his fingers through his steel-gray crew cut. "This one should be a piece of cake with a cherry on top. These losers took only two games this season, but desperate teams can sometimes sneak up on you. Get careless and they win. They win, it gives us three losses and we are tied for the division championship. We win we get a nice rest before playoffs. Make that happen, boy."

Coach Buck slapped Connor on the back and sent him on his way. The late arrival on the field by the wide receiver was noted by a few fans. Connor heard some soft boos. He deserved this, too, but tuned out the noise and concentrated on the warm-up. Still, his eyes drifted toward where his parents, back from the British Isles, sat right down in front, not up in the sky boxes. Stevie, dressed in bright red and a sight to behold, sat between them. His family was here, together, and that was all that mattered. He went back to his stretches.

The Sinners won the toss. Minutes into the first quarter, Joe Dean handed off the ball to his halfback, Fullerton, who moved through a hole made by the offensive line big enough to drive maybe not a Mack truck but at least two Hummers through. Fullerton went down on the thirty-yard line.

On the next play, Joe arrowed a short pass to Deets. In the seconds it took Connor to wonder if Joe was protecting him by keeping him out of the action, Deets was brought down, his hands barely on the ball. The pigskin rolled free and Connor Riley covered it. Two opposing players piled on top. Connor's helmet came off.

The two opposing backs were on their feet. They looked at each other as if they wanted to do a high five. Getting Riley tossed from the game would give their team a small edge. Connor rose slowly and turned away from the camera. He took a breath so deep the expansion of his broad shoulders could be captured on film. He pivoted. The smaller of the two backs stepped away.

The larger one held his ground and growled soft enough to be unheard by the officials, “Just doing my job, Riley. Want to make something of it, Goldilocks?”

“Like you said, you did your job and I did mine. We still have the ball.” Connor trotted off to join the huddle. He had something he wanted to say to Joe Dean Billodeaux before he called the play.

The action began again. The two backs covering Riley found themselves shoved off course while Connor slid into the end zone, caught Billodeaux’s easy arcing pass, spiked the ball in triumph and walked casually off the field.

Ancient Andy on his way to kick the extra point gave Riley a thumbs up. The Rev punched Connor’s arm lightly. Joe Dean took a seat on the bench next to his wide receiver. Coach Buck, watching the football soar over the crossbar, muttered a low key, “Nice work” in passing. Connor refrained from looking for his family. He had no need. On the big screens mounted near the top of the dome, Stevie, his mother and dad hugged.

The game was a rout, 49-zip. Connor added three touchdowns to his credit. The Rev scored one on a brilliant interception causing Al and Hank up in the booth to remark he was worth every penny the Sinners had spent to get him. Deets had a touchdown and Fullerton, passing through another hole big enough to fly a 737 through, ran the length of the field and scored without a man near him.

****

The sport analysts were dissecting the win before the team came out of the showers. Hank said, “Well, as Yogi used to say, that was déjà vu all over again. Connor Riley on the bottom of a pile, the helmet comes off, but does he fight? Not this time.”

“The outcome of the game is no surprise at least. The Sinners have been clear-cut division leaders for most of the season. But what do you think?" Al said to Hank. "Have we seen the comeback of wide receiver, Connor Riley?"

"I think Riley got more support from his team than any time since he started costing them yardage. As for Riley himself, the playoffs will give us the answer to that. Meanwhile, I'd say the Sinners are going to have a very happy New Year."

****

Connor insisted they go to the post-game celebration party, not so much because he wanted to, but because he needed to repair some more of the damage he had done, he told Stevie. Expecting a cold greeting, she protested all the way that she would rather have returned home with Keith and Kristen.

Clothed head to foot in Sinners' red, Stevie had purchased the spandex jumpsuit the day before the game at the Frederick's of Hollywood shop in the Quarter, surely the chosen shopping place of hookers and female impersonators. The shoes to match with six-inch ice pick heels held on by a complex crisscross of straps were on sale. In for a dollar, in for a dime. If the game seats had been on the upper tiers, she would have crawled up the narrow steps on hands and knees rather than risk a life-threatening plunge to the lower decks because of her footwear. She wore her straight blonde hair—longer than ever because she had neglected to get it cut while moping along on the golf tour—loose and capless so Connor would be able to see her face and pick out the red jumpsuit in the crowd. Hair in her face, spandex climbing into her crotch, feet aching, overall Stevie was miserably uncomfortable. The things we do for love.

Connor got playful on the drive to the celebration. While she adored seeing him this way, Stevie thought she had gone too far in an attempt give him encouragement. He kept pulling the gold ring on the long front zipper of the jumpsuit down inch by inch until the lace edging on the red Victoria's Secret pushup bra, another regrettable purchase, showed along with a great deal of cleavage. Stevie pulled the zipper up two inches. He pulled it down an inch. They arrived at the club before she could make another adjustment.

Connor drew her from the car and tucked her against his body as tightly as he carried a football. They became part of the throng together. Other players shook Connor's hand or gave him a back slap. No one said anything much to Stevie until Joe Dean materialized through the alcohol fumes and shadows.

He swallowed and said huskily, "Lookin' fine, Stevie. Ah...come sit with the Rev and me."

Dr. Arminta Green sat at their table. She had changed from the jeans and Sinner's shirt worn at the game into a classic little black dress accented with tiny bits of gold on her ears, neck and wrist. She wore sensible low sandals that Stevie envied. The Rev's engagement ring weighed down her slim hand. She took in Stevie's attire and let out a great bubbling laugh.

"I know. It's way over the top." Stevie apologized for her lame effort at being sexy.

"Ignore her," the Rev boomed. "You hot, girl. Where can I get my Mintay an outfit like that for the Super Bowl?"

"Don't worry. I won't tell him," Stevie assured Arminta who laughed some more.

Joe Dean poured champagne all around from the bottle in its ice bucket on the center of the table. He muttered over his own glass, "Seven more weeks, maybe less."

A tall, bony woman, her hair dyed the peculiar purple-red of henna, stalked over to their group on her very own stiletto heels. She had gone braless beneath her low-cut dress in a shiny snakeskin print but showed more jutting collarbone and ribs than breast. Clearly, she wanted something. Joe Dean reached in his jacket pocket, took out his leather book and a pen. Stevie just shook her head at his never-ending string of women.

In a low voice meant to be seductive but sounding more like a bad sinus condition, the woman introduced herself. "I'm Margaret Stutes from the PR department."

Joe Dean flipped his book to the "S" section. "Well, Margaret, you're already in here, sugar. You can't sign twice. Sorry. I have to spread myself around after my celibacy ends, but I'll be in touch."

Margaret settled herself in the chair opposite his seat, and Joe took off. He appeared to be crossing out a name in his book as he went. Margaret leaned over the table toward her next target and gave Connor a look down her top. He pushed his chair back abruptly and stood up. "I've got to circulate, too, Margaret. Nice meeting you."

"Me, too," said the Rev, not taking any chances. He followed Connor from the table.

"So it's just us girls now. You know, I had to come here with a reserve defensive lineman," she complained, disgust in her voice. "With my publicity skills, I could make or break these guys, but do they appreciate me? No." She helped herself to Joe Dean's unfinished champagne, drained the glass and shoved it into her rather large evening bag. "Souvenir," she explained. "You with Connor Riley? Good looking in a blond sort of way but very moody. I like mine dark and lively," she confided to Stevie.

"Margaret, I've been meaning to come to see you about that job offer. I'm Stevie Dowd, the photographer."

"Oh, I thought you were some bimbo the Barbarian picked up. Didn't recognize you without your gear. I can't say we have any openings right now. No onc has asked about you lately," Margaret said in the voice of a woman who regularly practiced bitchery and knew when a person was at her mercy.

"I need to travel with the team and keep busy during the games. Sitting in the stands waiting for something to happen doesn't agree with me. I could be of more use down on the field." Stevie tried to keep the pleading out of her voice, but Margaret's sharp PR trained ears heard her desperation.

"Well, you and Joe Dean are tight, right? If you could get him to start with Stutes, Margaret, at the end of the season when he gives up this celibacy shit, there might be a place for you." Margaret waited like a boa constrictor sizing up a tethered goat.

"I couldn't. Yes, I could. I need to be with Connor."

"You won't be able to sleep with him. They lock the team up tight during playoffs and the Super Bowl."

"That doesn't matter. I need to be on the field doing my job."

"The deal is what I said, and I need to hear it from Joe's own mouth."

"I'll try."

Dr. Arminta Green shook her head sadly.

****

Across the room far from where the all black rhythm and blues band wailed out slow and sexy dance tunes, Joe, Connor and the Rev huddled.

"No one's talking to Stevie. By now, we should have had half a dozen guys over at the table," Connor said to his friends. "All we've attracted is that PR barracuda."

"My Mintay will stand by her," the Rev asserted proudly.

"It's my fault. I've been blaming her for your acting out. Let me see what I can do. You guys go be charming to the team owner or something." Joe Dean put on his brightest smile and approached a group of linemen.

"Great work today." He slung an arm around a

set of beefy shoulders. "Stevie is back. Connor is on track, and I say we are going to the Super Bowl."

"Today was too easy, man. Not even much of a game, but yeah, it was good to see Connor in action now that Steel-hearted Stevie, the stone cold bitch, is back in town. No man should be so whipped," the nose tackle said.

"Right on," agreed the tight end.

"I see it this way. I got my holy medal. The Rev's got a cross. Connor has Stevie as his good luck charm. Besides, she tells me she left because she couldn't stand to see Connor injured again."

"My wife worries, too, but she don't tell me how to earn my living. Doesn't complain about our income, neither," the tight end added gruffly.

"We need Connor at his best if we have to take on the Patriots again, so let's give Stevie another chance, my friends. Just having the best defense in the league won't do it." Joe slapped a few backs and went on to the next group.

The tight end looked at the nose tackle. "Go ask her to dance."

"Why I got to do everything. I'm none too light on my feet."

"Just go."

Stevie watched the gigantic defense player make his way to her table. He settled in front of her like a huge pile of coal. "Miss Stevie, I'm Calvin Armitage, nose tackle for the Sinners defense."

"The best in the league," Stevie answered showing she knew very well who he was.

Calvin beamed in a way that said maybe she wasn't such a stone cold bitch after all. "May I have the pleasure of this dance?"

"Ah, sure." Stevie wobbled to her feet and, giving Mintay a puzzled look, followed Calvin to the dance floor. She took advantage of the screen of his bulk to pull her zipper up another inch. They trundled around the other couples to the tune of *When a Man Loves a Woman* until the tight end had mercy and cut in.

"Asa Dobbs here to protect you from Curse 'Em and Crush 'Em Calvin, Stevie," he said smoothly.

The Rev sailed by with Mintay. He was holding her close and whispering in her ear. Stevie searched for Connor, her eyes just above Asa's shoulder. She saw Margaret fuming alone at the table, but no sign of Connor or Joe.

After three successive dances during which she seemed to have met most of the defensive and offensive lines, Joe Dean cut in. "I am here to rescue you from the heavy-footed. Joe Dean treads on no woman." He twirled her around and drew her back into his arms. "Having fun?"

"I'm not the best dancer either, but they don't seem to feel it when I tread on *them*. Joe, I have the biggest, most enormous favor to ask of you as Connor's friend." She could feel the quarterback tense beneath the hand she had around his back.

"You're asking what?"

Stevie took a deep breath. "I'm asking you to start with Margaret Stutes at the end of the season."

"But, Stevie, *mon amour*, that would not be fair to the other ladies who wait. I was going to start with the A's or maybe the Z's. Even then, Barbara Zelinsky, Sue Yablonsky, and Latasha Xavier, a very hot college chick, would have first chance."

"I need to be with Connor during the playoffs, down on the field near him. I cannot sit still anymore and wait for things to happen. I need to be involved. Margaret can get me a photography job with the Sinners. I'm sorry to ask. She wants to hear from your lips that she will be first before she'll help me." Stevie looked up at him with tear-glazed eyes.

"Oh, hell, why does it matter where I start? I can take one for the team and for Connor."

Still, Stevie felt the quarterback shudder as

Margaret gave him a small wave and a big smile complete with overbite from the sidelines. He steered Stevie her way and mouthed over her red-spandexed shoulder, "You're number one, Maggie."

Margaret Stutes pointed a finger at him and said right back, "And don't you dare forget it."

The band took a break. The team owner seized control of the microphone to announce a bonus for taking the division championship and to promise big rewards if the Sinners won the Super Bowl. Amid cheers and "right-ons," Mintay steered Stevie to one of the quieter tables where a group of team wives sat smartly garbed in Saks Fifth Avenue—as opposed to Stevie's tacky Frederick's of Hollywood ensemble as they could get. Dr. Green had taken some of her very precious and limited spare time to get to know these women and she introduced Stevie to the ladies.

"So you are the lady who brought Connor Riley to his knees. That almost cost us the division crown," said Sharlette Dobbs, putting a little sting in her voice.

"I left him because after his injury, I wanted him to give up football. As you can see, that didn't work. I'm, ah—wearing this outfit so he could see me in the stands rooting for him today." Stevie was willing to shoulder all the blame for Connor's slump and never reveal otherwise, but the clothes she felt she had to explain.

"The things we do for our men! I used to run around the house in a red lace teddy…four children and sixty pounds ago," Mrs. Calvin Armitage recalled with a soulful look at her large bosom and back toward her equally large behind. She was so tastefully dressed she might have taken lessons from Oprah Winfrey.

"Cal says it takes a big woman to be his lover and bear more tackles, bless his heart, but I wouldn't have the nerve to ask him to give up football. You have courage, girl. I could tell that when you danced with my husband. How are the feet doing, baby?"

"Killing me," Stevie said laughing. "But mostly because I usually wear running shoes."

"I guess I might be a tad envious of you. During the season, Ace wouldn't notice if I took off and spent a month in Barbados. Sometimes, I do," confessed Sharlette. "I worry about him and he just blows me off. He makes up for it in the spring, though."

"We all worry. We all have that in common," Mintay added. "You're not alone, Stevie."

"Amen to that," Precious Armitage pronounced.

The band returned refreshed and ready to do another set. They started up with a fast and heavy beat. Calvin Armitage made his way to the table and pulled his wife from her chair. "I have rediscovered the joy of dance, sweet thang."

"Just so you keep your joy off my feet, teddy bear," Precious responded as they boogied away.

Two large, long-fingered hands came to rest on Stevie's shoulders. She knew his touch. "Where have you been, Connor?"

"Mingling, my dear." He kissed the top of her head. "Let's dance."

"Where is Ace when I want him?" Sharlette sighed.

"I think he's in the bar watching replays," the Rev answered her as he claimed Mintay.

"Figures. It's still football season."

****

Stevie, heavy-eyed, was grateful to be wrapped by Connor's warm arm as they drove back to the north shore. The killer red shoes had done major damage to her feet and lay under the seat of the car where she had kicked them. Connor worked her zipper down again and rested his hand on her breast.

Was that dawn backlighting the cypress trees? "The only thing I want right now is a toe rub," she confessed.

"Me, too. We have a nice break before the next game except for training and team meetings. First playoff game will be played here. No travel time for us."

"Speaking of which, I asked Margaret Stutes to get me photo credentials for the games. I'll be there for all of them. I don't want to just sit and watch. I love your mother, but we make each other even more anxious. By the way, Joe Dean sacrificed himself for this. We owe him big time."

"I could have asked for the credentials. No need to involve Joe."

"But then you would have been the one who had to sleep with Margaret."

"Like hell! I would have asked her boss, but the way Joe Dean goes through women, he'll probably get over it pretty fast. Still, Margaret Stutes—I do owe him."

"Some of the wives I met tonight were nice. They worry about their husbands, too."

"Good."

"Mintay introduced me around. That probably made a difference. She's very well liked. They were kind to me despite my being dressed like a hooker."

"You looked great. Not a guy in the room could take his eyes off you."

"Yours were the only eyes I cared about." He gave her one of those smiles that melted her insides and made her forget her worries.

"I enjoyed Christmas with your family, Connor. Your mom and I talked. She understands why I left…your dad, too."

"Merrilee and Kevin's kids weren't too much for you?"

"Christmas is more fun with children around. I got some great shots of them dumping their stockings and opening their gifts, playing with the toys. Maybe if I make up a small album and give it to Merrilee I can win her over."

"Don't bother trying. She will always be jealous. Once when I was still playing college ball, she came on to me when Kevin was out of town. She was about three months pregnant with Katie and said no one would ever know, but she had to get even with my brother because she knew he was away cheating on her. I laughed it off as a hormone attack—which did not make her happy. I may have lusted after my brother's college girlfriend, but I would never sleep with my brother's wife."

"Good to know it." Stevie drifted, wondering if that was all there was to it—lust and competition with his brother now that he knew the real Stephanie, not the ideal one he had a crush on in high school. Since her return, Connor had not repeated his proposal or said the words of love. She closed her eyes, slept, and missed hearing what she had been waiting for since her return.

"I love you, Stevie Dowd."

Chapter Twenty-Two

Like a hot knife through butter, like shit through a goose, like every cliché for something quick and easy, the Sinners cut down each team on their path to the Super Bowl. When they packed their bags and headed to the great new stadium in Houston, Stevie went with them. Knowing Connor's time would be monopolized with pre-game hype and training, she stayed with her sister.

Her brother-in-law, Brent, completely forgave Connor for his antics on the field when Stevie handed over her lone ticket. She had her press pass and didn't need it. After declaring Connor Riley the greatest wide receiver of all time—he had gone through a rough patch, that was all—Brent asked, "If he becomes my brother-in-law, do you think we could get two tickets next time? Then you could go along, Michelle, honey."

Michelle snorted, but their mother inquired sourly, "Yes, how is that going?"

"If the Sinners make it to another Super Bowl, I will try to get three tickets. Okay, everyone?" Stevie answered, pretending to misunderstand.

"Don't evade me, Stephanie. I know you are living with that man. Your security deposit refund on the New Orleans house was mailed here." Mrs. Dowd waved an open envelope containing a check in Stevie's face. "Knowing your record with men and that football player's nasty disposition, don't you think you should make it legal before something goes wrong?"

Stevie winced. She had forgotten she'd used

Michelle's address for forwarding. Though difficult to give up her independence, Stevie had notified her landlord she was moving—an attempt to give Connor total commitment. This concession had not gone exactly as planned. Impulsively, she'd hired a one-day mover and had all of her belongings sitting in a van in the driveway when Connor returned from a practice session.

"Honey," he'd said carefully. "Where were you planning to put all this stuff?"

Some very expensive vehicles sat out in the weather while she sorted through the boxes. The majority of her furnishings and household goods, none of them as fine as the ones chosen by Connor's decorator, went to the Salvation Army. Her photography equipment, the best she could afford, now took up two parking places in the air-conditioned garage as she waited for the promised studio to be built. Connor told her to go ahead and find a contractor, tell him what she wanted and send the bill to him, but Stevie felt hesitant to do so. She wasn't doing studio work right now. She could wait to see how things went between them.

"Mother, I am very serious about Connor. He had some problems. We both did, but now things are better. He's honest with me, generous and kind."

"And he has a great body," Michelle chipped in.

"That, too," Stevie admitted.

"When he gets tired of you, you'll be out on the street with nowhere to go and nothing to show for your time," her mother warned.

"Mom, I have a job of my own."

"With the Sinners. How long will that last if he moves on to someone else? You know how these athletes are."

"I'll be careful. Look, I have to get to the stadium and do some PR pictures. A few of the players are meeting some of the Louisiana Wish Kidz who wanted to attend the Super Bowl."

"Well, that's no Olympic assignment," her mother huffed.

"No, but I still have to go." Glad of the excuse, Stevie grabbed her gear and headed out to the stadium. Her consolation prize, Connor, would be there.

****

In one of the luxury suites of Reliant Stadium, Connor Riley, Joe Dean Billodeaux and Rev Bullock waited for the Wish Kidz to arrive. Joe stayed in the box since skinny Margaret Stutes lurked like a witch who devoured small children in the hallway near the elevator and waited to greet the sick kids.

He looked out over 69,500 empty seats toward the field being groomed to perfection. "Tomorrow is the day. Tomorrow, the Sinners win the Super Bowl," he said tossing one of the autographed footballs destined for the sick children from hand to hand. "My long, long fast will be over. Ladies, look out."

The Rev shook his head sadly over the comment and helped himself to the complimentary barbecued shrimp and bacon wrapped chicken livers, took a long swig from a bottle of fizzy water. He left the breaded chicken nuggets and tiny wieners with the dipping sauce for the kids. Fastidiously, he wiped his big fingers on a napkin and took care not to get any grease on the team jersey he wore over street clothes. At the end of the meeting each child would get a jersey actually worn by their heroes.

Connor, dressed in his black game shirt with the red 80 on the back, drank chocolate milk from a small bottle, got a brown milk mustache, and was wiping his lips on a napkin when Stevie came through the door preceded by a tiny woman not much bigger than a child. Joe Dean watched Connor glance over the delicate lady and lock with Stevie's gaze. She raised her camera and clicked. That Stevie, camera always in hand to catch the moment.

No woman had ever given him the kind of loving look she shared with Connor.

The small woman continued on and positioned herself in front of the players. Joe Dean swiveled in his seat. He didn't know how she got in here, but everyone in the room knew what she wanted. Even the cute, spiky-haired blonde with the dragon tattoo who brought in the refreshments had signed his fabled book and hinted she would be around after the game. He gave this petite woman with the big, dark eyes a dazzling grin and pulled the black book from his pocket.

Standing on the steps, Stevie eyed Connor again and sighed. Joe Dean knew what she was thinking. Billodeaux is a sex addict—but he'd stayed celibate for the entire season, more than Connor could say.

"Here you go, sugar. What's your name, sweetheart?" he asked as he picked up one of the felt-tipped pens used to autograph the footballs.

"Nellwyn Abbott," she replied, returning his attention with a cordial smile.

"Abbott. Why you go right to the top of my list, Nellie. You just beat out Lacey Abshire for first place with Joe Dean Billodeaux."

Coming up beside Stevie, Margaret Stutes glared at him from the entry. Joe Dean ignored her and concentrated on the fine, delicate lady before him. Not his type as he was usually seen with bigger women all away around, but Joe denied no female the chance to leave her name. Behind him, the Rev cleared his throat loud enough for everyone in the room to hear.

Was that going to stop him? No. He continued with the seductive business at hand. "Now, how can I get in touch with you after the game? You live here in town?"

"No. No, I don't. We came in from New Orleans. I'm a Sinners fan, too, of course, but—"

"Even better, sugar. I can get to you soon as we

get back to the state with our trophy. That would be area code 504, right?"

"Yes, but—"

The Rev's voice attempting to interrupt grew louder. He was going into preacher mode. Connor laughed so hard, he had lowered his head on to his arms. The Rev blasted out as if he were standing at his father's pulpit, "Joe Dean, you hitting on the Wish Lady."

Joe blinked. Tiny fingers tipped with pale, pink-polished nails laid a business card on the well-filled "A" page of his little black book. It read, "Nellwyn Abbott, Volunteer, Louisiana Wish Kidz Foundation."

On the landing, Margaret mouthed, "I'm first" to the stunned Joe Dean. Behind her stood a group of parents and children—a frail little boy in a wheelchair, a black child whose joints were bigger than the limbs surrounding them, a pale girl bespeckled with freckles. The last child wore a black Sinner's bandanna twisted around her bald head like a gang member. The intent was to look tough but came across more like a piece of a pirate costume. Blue-coated disability service team members flanked the children.

Stevie clicked her camera and captured Joe's slack-jawed look on film along with the small, serene smile of the Wish Lady, her hand on the black book, and Joe Dean's total humiliation. Damn that Stevie Dowd.

Connor, always quick with a recovery, pushed a note pad toward the quarterback. "Let's sign a few autographs for our guests, Joe."

"Sure, sure. Wish Lady, Miss Abbott, Nellie, how would you like your autograph to read?" Joe Dean did have the basic decency to be embarrassed.

"To Nell, not Nellie," she laughed softly. "I will never forget this moment."

That's exactly how the autograph came out, "To

Nell—not Nellie—I will never forget this moment. Joe Dean Billodeaux, Sinner." He drew a line under his name ending with a devil's tail looping around to form a heart. Inside the heart, he wrote his phone number.

Grinning again, he said as he handed the paper over to Nellwyn Abbott, "But give it some thought."

"I am sure most women would be honored, but I'm here for the children. Let me introduce you."

Seeing that the wheelchair might be a problem, Joe Dean rose and went to shake hands with his audience. Connor and the Rev followed, still snickering like brothers who caught a sibling making out with his girlfriend.

"This is Patrick Maguire and Willie Jones and Cassie Thomas," Nell introduced. "Each one picked their favorite player to meet."

"I guess I'm yours," Joe Dean said to the girl who looked to be about thirteen. He was doomed to be embarrassed again.

"Oh, no! Mr. Connor is mine. He's so beautiful," she sighed. "Not that you aren't sexy Mr. Joe, but I want a man who will pine for his one true love like he did for Stevie Dowd. Say, did you just hit on Miss Nellwyn?"

"We often call her Sassy," said Nellwyn Abbott.

Behind Cassie, her flustered mother fluttered her hands. "I don't know where she gets these ideas."

"From that newspaper you always buy at the grocery store, Mom. Didn't you see it a couple of weeks ago when we were picking our favorite players? The headline said *Sweetheart Stevie Returns, Riley Rises.* "

"Oh good Lord! I'll never buy that rag again. I'm so sorry, Mr. Riley," Mrs. Thomas blurted. It was easy to see where Cassie had gotten her freckles and probably red hair and a quick blush, too, when she was well.

"I can't complain if it's true," Connor answered

graciously.

"So, who gets me?" asked Joe Dean turning the conversation back to himself.

"I do," the wheelchair-bound child said eagerly.

Joe Dean pulled off his jersey and put it over the boy's extended arms. "This is for you. We have an autographed football, too. How about I get you out of this chair and carry you down by the front window so we can scope out the field and have some eats. They tell me the Sinners have donated this box for y'all and your families."

Patrick Maguire's thin and worried mother gasped as if her son might shatter during transport, but the boy with the huge jersey pooling around his hips held up his arms again and gave Joe a smile full of hero worship. Joe Dean lifted the child who was so light his bones seemed to be filled with air and carried him with ease to a regular seat.

The Rev turned to Willie. "You must be mine, son. Climb on my back, we all going for a ride."

The black child, who looked like a starving refugee from Africa, put his arms around the big man's neck and his toothpick legs around his waist.

Connor gallantly offered his arm to Cassie who accepted, too shameless with adoration to match her mother's blush. The procession moved toward the food tables. Stevie snapped the heart-warming pictures that would be in the paper and on the Sinners' web site the next day. Really, nothing was wrong with heart-warming.

Chapter Twenty-Three

Game day, Stevie wandered, filling her cameras with pictures of pre-game preparations. The dome was closed against the weather, but she found the real grass comforting. Connor had told her a grass field meant fewer injuries. This year's theme ran towards country/western patriotic. Some big star would yodel out the national anthem. A live eagle was scheduled to be released for a flight back to its trainer's hand. Celebrities filled the stands if they wanted to be seen and the luxury suites if they did not. Stevie found the sameness to last year's event unnerving. She kept her mind off of it by doing her job.

Before the action started, she stopped by the Riley family box and exchanged fervent hugs with Kris Riley that only the two women truly understood. Keith Riley was there being a good grandfather. He had taken the older children over to the NFL Experience earlier and now plied everyone with hot dogs to settle them down. Kevin bickered with Merrilee about her breast-feeding nine-month old Courtney right there under a Sinners blanket.

"For God's sake, Merrilee, the child is walking and has teeth. Give it up."

"You know I always breast-feed for at least a year, Kevin, sometimes until the age of two. It's good for the baby. What do you think, Stevie?"

Stevie threw up her hands. "No opinion. No opinion whatsoever, but I'll take a mother/daughter picture if you like," and she did, making her escape back to the field soon afterwards where the tension seemed more bearable.

"Stefania, *bella* Stefania, over here." Marcello, of course. Marcello had to be here to make things perfect. He had his arm around the model, Amber.

"I like the American football very much last year. So much more dangerous than soccer games. Your fella, the man I see you with, he is good to play, eh? I gotta big bet on the Sinners. The Amberello Agency, she is doing good. I pay for my tickets this year. And hey, see this. We make our own little football."

Marcello pulled the ever elegant Amber from her seat and turned her sideways. He patted her round, tight tawny belly with its protruding navel poking out between low-slung jeans and a snug red midriff-baring top.

"Oh, you two have gotten married since I saw you in Italy! Congratulations," Stevie shouted up at them.

"No, no, marriage is for peasants. We are business partners. We make a beautiful baby. She will be a model like her mother. Maybe we name her Stefania."

Amber's beautiful almond-shaped eyes narrowed. She pulled her top down and her pants up from where they rested on her narrow hips. Her navel still protruded. "We are naming her Gabriella," she spit. "And if I have one stretch mark you will be forever sorry."

"Yes, yes, I will be, *cara mia*." Marcello soothed her with words, but his expression said he already was.

"Good luck to you two, then." Stevie waved and moved on. At least the baby was not Joe Dean's offspring. She would tell him about his fortunate escape after the game. Might make him think harder about using all the names in his little black book.

She was hailed from another section of the stands with a whistle and a loud yell.

"Baby doll! Up here!" Jackie Haile leaned over a railing. "I told that ass, Joe Dean, I could afford my own tickets, but I'm rooting for him anyhow."

"Great to see you, Jackie. Is that your father with you?"

"Ah, yes. We reconciled. Isn't it great?" Jackie poked her father in the ribs with an elbow.

The stocky, gray-haired man who looked like an old version of Jackie said, "Our reconciliation was long overdue. I love my girl." He added an impromptu hug.

"Jackie, thanks. I wouldn't be here today if you hadn't talked to me back in Vegas," Stevie shouted through cupped hands.

"Yeah, well. You can name your firstborn after me," the golfer replied a little uncomfortably.

"That's a promise," Stevie vowed.

She turned and bumped into Dexter Sykes. Since she had been covering the playoff games, he seemed to dog her steps. Dex tweaked her about giving up the New Orleans studio. "I guess as a lowly photographer I didn't make enough bucks to keep us together," he had the nerve to say.

"I guess as a lowly photographer, you didn't have enough integrity to keep us together, Dex. I haven't forgiven you for selling those shots of me to *Sports Illustrated* last year."

"Baby, you signed the model's release. Those pictures opened up a whole new field for me, too. Guess who gets to work on the swimsuit issue next year?"

"Dexter Sykes, naturally." Stevie rolled her eyes.

"Dexter Sykes on an island with the world's most beautiful women and you made it all possible, Stevie girl. Tell that hulk you're living with if he wants any more copies, they're on the house."

She had nothing more to say to or about Dexter Sykes. She would never collaborate with him again.

Except at the publicity events going on all week

long, the one person she had seen little of was Connor Riley. Sequestered in their team hotel at night, phone calls had been their only private contact. Connor seemed distracted, his mind on the game and coping with any fears he might have. She could listen if he wanted to talk, but that was all. She would be here on the field dealing with her own fears, little enough to offer to him.

Missing from this year's lineup—Connor's nemesis, Damon Suggs. Joe Dean had told her in a quick aside at the Wish Kidz meeting that Suggs had been traded away to a lesser team. The Patriots played tough, but they disliked Suggs' attitude. Some had talked about banning him from the league after the spearing incident, but the difficulty lay in proving the move was intentional and not simply an over-eager attempt to tackle by a novice player. Intimidating men like Suggs had their value, especially to teams without a strong defense.

Fans who had paid over a thousand dollars for a ticket to this event watched two teams so evenly matched the game went scoreless well into the second quarter. Both quarterbacks suffered sacks handed out by ferocious defensive lines. They battled for feet, not yards. Joe Dean was unable to reach any of his wide receivers whether they played two or three in the backfield. Stevie trolled the sidelines attempting to get some exciting snaps, but nothing much turned up.

A break came when the Rev saved the Sinners' bacon with an interception on the Pats thirty-yard line. The best his team was able to do was move within field goal range before the half ended. Knowing the fans remembered his failed kick in last year's bowl, Ancient Andy took his place behind the ball.

Sinners' crowd fell silent. Patriots' backers created a ruckus to shake the kicker. Stevie knew Andy Mortenson had considered retirement and stayed on because Connor Riley asked him to stick around. "We'll get 'em next year, Andy, I promise." That, coming from a man flat on his back with a broken neck, made a quiet slip into obscurity seem like cowardice. This one would be for Connor Riley. Stevie captured the perfect calm and equilibrium of the grizzled kicker as he addressed the ball.

The pigskin arched up and over the outstretched arms of the tallest defenders and cleared the bar with feet to spare. The signal for halftime sounded. As the teams jogged back to their locker rooms, the players buffeted Ancient Andy with backslaps and pulled him along with handshakes. Stevie stood close enough to hear Connor say said in passing, "Glad you stayed with us, Andy." He might not have won the game, but the picture of that kick told a story of redemption.

While the teams rested and the coaches plotted the second half, men and women in black or white cowboy hats strutted on to the stage. Tight black T-shirts and jeans attired the men while the female performers wore lots of fringe barely covering their breasts and long sequined pants riding just above their pubic areas, country/western gone Britney Spears. Stevie, wishing the spectacle was over, wishing the entire game was over, drank from a water bottle and did her job.

Both teams came back with renewed energy and new strategies. The Pats slugged their way down the field and scored early in the third quarter. Billodeaux tried to return the favor. He stood like a rock amid the crashing bodies falling around him, sighted on Connor and threw his long pass.

Connor rose up to receive the ball, connected, and was slammed down hard by one of the two backs covering him. Stevie froze. Connor got up and wiped his hands on the small red towel at his waist as he searched the sidelines. When he found her, he gave a slight wave telling her he was fine. The crowd took the wave as their own, applauded and started coursing it around the stadium, but Stevie knew he had thrown her a lifeline and they were holding each other steady on both ends of it.

The first half had been easy on Connor with Joe unable to deliver his passes. The Sinners' halfback took much of the heat and Joe himself ran the ball a couple of times when no receivers came open. Cameras in the locker room caught Coach Buck cautioning Joe Dean during the break, "Don't get hurt, boy. Trust your line and get those passes out." Good advice, Stevie thought, if only Joe could follow it.

Billodeaux visibly tried to act on that advice, but his next pass to Deets was batted down. The next, also to Deets, intercepted and run back to the fifty-yard line. The defense held the Pats to a field goal, score 3-10.

Stevie wondered if Joe Dean was being soft on Connor or were the two backs stalking his favorite wide receiver really keeping him from passing in that direction? Billodeaux back-stepped, faked towards Deets, swiveled and shot the ball to Riley. Connor moved toward the goal line, then reversed and plunged through a gap between the defenders to snatch the ball from the air. Both backs brought him down hard on his face but the ball rested on the twenty-yard line. Connor sat up, not rising immediately.

Coaches and medics pushed past Stevie on their way to the field. They helped Connor up and back to the bench, but his head turned in Stevie's direction. She saw his nod through the viewfinder of the camera she used to cover the two tears running down her face. She swabbed her face with the long sleeve of the red Sinners jersey, a souvenir item bearing Conner's number eighty on the back, covered from sight by her photographer's vest.

Coach replaced Riley with the young receiver,

Forte, and the rookie got the honors as Billodeaux fired one into the end zone to tie the game, 10-10, going into the fourth quarter. The clock ran down. Neither team scored. The Sinners held the ball with two minutes to play. Coach Buck sent Riley back in along with Deets and Forte to dilute the defense and give Joe Dean as many targets as possible. Acting as superstitious as Joe Dean, Stevie sucked in her breath and crossed her fingers

Billodeaux completed two short passes to Deets, pulling the defense over to his side of the field, and called a last time out. After much conferring and shaking of heads, Joe came back to the line of play. Deets seemed to be his chosen receiver again, but Joe Dean lobbed one instead to Forte in the center of the field. Goal defenders surged towards Forte, two from his right, one from his left. He hesitated instead of running, then threw a lateral to Connor Riley who had moved up stealthily a few yards from Forte. His guard, caught facing Forte, failed to intercept as Connor connected, surged forward, deflected a last minute tackle with a strong back kick and crossed the goal line.

Time ran out and stood still as Connor Riley, holding the ball high, passed beneath the goal posts and kept on running. He spiked the football, but did not stop. Stevie Dowd stood beyond the end zone letting Connor fill the frame of her camera. She caught his triumphant spring under the goal post, his spike of the ball, the golden hair on his shoulders, the determined look on the face beneath the helmet he tore off as he kept coming. He reached forward, seized Stevie by the waist, and swung her around and around.

Her camera flew back across her shoulder on its strap. Her feet left the ground and even her ponytail could not keep the black Sinners cap on her head. Laughing, she said, "Connor Riley, you are a thing of beauty. Now put me down before you get fined for excessive celebration."

"They won't fine me tonight. Stevie Dowd, I love you. Are you willing to marry a Super Bowl winner?"

"I would marry Connor Riley, any time, any place, in any condition and without any reservations."

The long, long kiss went largely unnoticed among the people in the celebrating crowd on the field, but was caught on national television and by Dexter Sykes who always got good shots when his ex-girlfriend was involved. Dex snapped away while Connor and Stevie ignored him. These pics might be too mushy and sentimental for *Sports Illustrated*, but the tabloids or even *People* magazine would love to have it on their covers. Stevie had truly set him on the road to a new career.

Dex followed the sports reporters as they advanced into the fray, microphones held before them like lances. They captured Coach Buck up on the big screen with his arm around Joe Dean Billodeaux.

"I can only say this boy has grown up right before my eyes. He has changed from a cocky, woman-chasing sonofabitch to one of the best quarterbacks in the league, a real leader who cares about his team and led them to this victory in the Super Bowl." The five-second delay omitted the questionable words and the mike moved towards Joe Dean.

"It's a privilege to play with great men like Connor Riley and Rev Bullock, old-timers like Andy Mortenson and new talent like DeVon Deets and Jared Forte. We've got the best linemen in the league, the best team in the league, and we just proved it! But ladies, I'm still a woman-chasing sonofabitch and I start again tonight." The networks deleted all of Joe's last remark.

On the edge of the crowd surrounding Joe Dean and the coach, Margaret Stutes lurked. She pointed a finger at the quarterback.

With Connor now standing next to him, Stevie in tow, Joe whispered, “Did you see that? I hope they got a whole case of champagne in the locker room with my name on it because that’s how much I need to keep my word to Margaret.”

The reporters homed in on Connor Riley like heat-seeking missiles. He pulled Stevie against his side when they surrounded him. “Think you will be voted Most Valuable Player, Connor?”

“I don’t deserve the honor. You can’t achieve a victory like this without a great friend and quarterback like Joe Dean Billodeaux, a fantastic team that gave me a second chance to come back, and the support of the ones you love the best.” He smiled down on Stevie Dowd.

“When’s the wedding, Stevie?” Rita Fortunado shouted out.

“Any time, any place, anywhere without any conditions,” she answered.

****

Up in the press box, Al Harney said to Hank Wilkes, “Well, this is the end of a story that started last season. Connor Riley gets my vote for MVP.”

“Not Joe Dean Billodeaux who had a fantastic season and undoubtedly argued for that last winning play?” questioned Hank.

“Billodeaux has come a long way this season, no doubt about it, but he is going to be with this team for many years. Riley came back from a horrendous accident last season and pulled out of a career damaging slump this season to make a major difference in this game. He exemplifies the best in football. As I said, he gets my vote.”

“And the hero gets the girl, Al.”

“A happy ending all around, Hank.”

Chapter Twenty-Four

New Age music on zithers or dulcimers or sitars twanged in Stevie's ears driving her slightly nuts. She raised one of the herbal teabags the facial technician had plunked on her eyes like pennies on a corpse right after placing a trowel full of goop called *cucumber moisturizing lotion* on Stevie's face. Scented candles flickered all around her in the dim room.

She looked down the row of five women stretched out flat to her left: Mintay, her two sisters, Sharlette Dobbs, and the mound of Precious Armitage on the very end. All wore thick, white terry robes, pale green facial masks, teabags and turbans to keep the stuff out of their hair. Paper flip-flops protected their fresh pedicures. Stevie had already blotched her freshly painted nails when she tried to get the restroom door open after too many cups of green tea. Oh well, fooling with her cameras would have done the same. She was supposed to be relaxing or meditating or something, but the whole scenario said "funeral" to her.

She sure hoped the team wives wouldn't give *her* a bachelorette party like this one with a morning at the spa, a three martini lunch to follow, then shopping, an evening at the House of Blues and maybe some time at the casino. Tick off the things Stevie Dowd did not enjoy and the only activity left would be the House of Blues. Still, she'd enjoyed the pedicure. Foot rubs stepped high up on the rungs of her pleasures. A second group of wives took theirs now while a third set went in for massages. Stevie's stomach growled. Lunch with or without the martinis would be welcome.

"I heard that," Precious Armitage said. "I'm rumbling, too. I could eat this stuff we got on our faces."

"No clocks in here. That German babe who gives the rough massages seized my watch on the way in, but I think we are almost done."

"Not enjoying yourself, Stevie? This is a real treat for me and I want to thank you, ladies," Mintay said. Like the Rev, she was always gracious. "Sorry I couldn't ask you to be in the wedding, but the Bullocks and the Greens have huge families full of girls who want to play dress up."

"That's okay. I never was much of a princess."

"But you are marrying a handsome prince of a man in June."

"Amen to that," Sharlette Dobbs, so often neglected by her own husband, said.

"I do have a special favor I'd like to ask of you." Mintay removed her teabags and turned her head slightly in Stevie's direction.

"I owe you for standing by me. What can I do for you?"

"Neutralize Joe Dean Billodeaux at my wedding."

"Ah, I don't think Connor would like that. Besides, Joe won't go off alone with the girlfriends or relatives of other players, married women or under-aged chicks. Virgins are also outside his limits, and still his little black book is full. Are you worried he will hit on the bridesmaids? None of them qualify for Joe."

"Now that's a damned shame," Mintay's older sister said.

"Kind of makes me wish I hadn't gotten married two years ago. Who knew my sister, the doctor, would marry a Sinner and open up a whole new field for me. Guess I will just have to be content with

Zack and my new baby," the bride's younger sister added.

"Zack is a fine man and your baby is precious. Be thankful for what you have as my fiancée would say. I didn't mean sleep with him, Stevie."

"Well, I can't castrate the guy either, much as I'd like to sometimes. Though, maybe Coach Buck would thank me. Joe's mind would be entirely on the game then."

"Stevie, you are awful yourself sometimes. No. I meant fix him up with a woman who will hold his attention, someone who won't fall into bed with him easily. Like the Wish Lady, the one who volunteers for the Louisiana Wish Kidz. Rev and I went to the funeral for little Willie Jones, and she was there. The Rev introduced me to her as the only woman who ever made Joe Dean go slack-jawed. He brought along a copy of that picture you took. Almost made us laugh at a very solemn occasion. Nell is small but she does have substance. I invited her to our wedding. How about her for Joe Dean? I think she could handle him since she's a child psychologist."

"Maybe. What do you care about Joe and his women?"

"Stevie, honey, I'm a doctor. I work long hours. I get called out at night for emergencies. Rev has time on his hands during the off-season. Joe hangs around with him and Connor and often brings along multiple women even on fishing trips, I'm told. Now, I trust my husband-to-be, but let's face it, sometimes men of the cloth do stray. Connor doesn't even have religious convictions to protect him from Joe Dean's doxies. We need to get that man married and settled."

Beneath the facial mask, Stevie's brow wrinkled. Not Connor, he would never cheat on her when he went fishing. Even at the lowest ebb of their relationship, neither had taken other lovers. Still…

"How do you want to work it?'

"You keep an eye out for her at the wedding. She did RSVP as a single, so no problem there. Rev says Joe called her after the Super Bowl and she turned him down again. Perfect. You save a seat for her right up front at your table. Run her by that dawg like a pork chop tied to a string. He won't be able to resist trying to catch the one who got away."

"I can do that." A timer went off. "Thank God," Stevie murmured.

The room flooded with attendants who wiped down the women and helped them off their padded slabs. They shuffled off in their robes and paper slippers like inmates in an asylum ready to escape, change clothes and reapply makeup before the big feed with alcoholic beverages at Brennan's restaurant.

****

Feeling a little bloated from the big lunch and mildly buzzed from all the liquor, Stevie held up the sleek, ice-blue evening gown she'd found on the sales rack at the very upscale store where the football wives had dragged her. "What do you think of this, Mintay?"

"For bridesmaids' dresses? You'd have to find several to match in different sizes. And I hate to admit, it's not my color. Now with those blue eyes and blonde hair and all that white skin, it suits you."

"I meant for me. You, my sister and Jackie can wear whatever you want as far as I'm concerned." For a moment, Stevie tried to envision stocky Jackie Haile in an evening gown. Nope, couldn't do it.

Sharlette Dobbs perused the price tag. "A good deal even if you don't wear it for your wedding. I'd buy it regardless, but try it on first. You never know 'til you get it on."

Stevie took her find into a dressing room, saw herself in the mirror and fell in love with the gown. Wearing low heels today and trying hard to fit in with the other wives, she raised the hem and strolled out to do a little model's strut past her audience of critics.

"Look, no need for strange underwear either."

"I hear you, baby," Precious Armitage said. "If I could get a dress to skim my hips that way I'd buy a dozen of 'em. But you do know the bridal department is right over there. Connor would spring for whatever you want, but you cutting it mighty close by setting a date the first week in June. Mintay's been working on her wedding since last summer.

"I love this dress. The rest of you can wear white. With higher heels, it doesn't need any alterations. Frankly, I wish Connor and I could just run off and get married quietly, but my mother would fuss and Mrs. Riley might feel cheated out of seeing her boy marry. At least, we are going to keep the ceremony private. Margaret Stutes and the PR department want a big blow-out reception. I told her to plan it."

"Oh, you shouldn't do that!" Mintay exclaimed. "That woman will make the reception hall look like the Jungle Room at Graceland with all her animal prints and such."

"No, I'll tell her pale blue linens to match this dress and daisies, lots of daisies. That sounds safe and simple, right? Say, maybe we could get Joe Dean to marry Margaret and spare the poor Wish Lady. She seems too nice to sacrifice on the Billodeaux altar. Margaret is obsessed with Joe, anyhow. Connor says he swears she knows everything about him: his stats, his list ladies, even Joe's license plate numbers and right down to the last penny he earned."

Mintay shook her head. "Rev says Joe finds Margaret repellent."

"Joe used a big word like repellent?"

"Well, he does hunt and fish and uses Deet. I think it says repellent on the can."

That set off the women. They doubled over

laughing, crushing their shopping bags to their chests and wiping their eyes.

"That was mean of me. My sweet man would say Joe Dean is cagey and smart but doesn't let people see that side of him. He swears the man has unplumbed depths."

"Yeah, but his biggest brain is in his pants," Sharlette Dobbs said.

"Joe Dean is about as deep as a kiddie pool," Precious added.

Each wife came up with another line about Joe Dean starting with "Joe Dean is…" as they paid for their purchases and left the store.

"Joe Dean is so horny, the New Orleans Symphony asked him to be the entire brass section."

"Joe Dean is such a lover he makes Casanova look like a librarian," Stevie improvised as they sat down for dinner crepes at Galatoire's in the French Quarter. The wives stared at her. "Too intellectual to be funny? See, Casanova *was* a librarian."

"I think we done drained the well of Joe Dean jokes," Precious said.

"But I believe we have made our point. Joe Dean Billodeaux needs a wife to rein him in," Mintay asserted. She wore a short, cheap bridal veil the other women had forced on her which made her the center of attention wherever they went.

"These are good," Stevie remarked digging into her food. "I think I need to tell Margaret I want crepes at the wedding. Where to next?"

"The House of Blues, baby." Precious held up her arms and waggled her substantial breasts.

At the nightclub, they shoved Mintay forward to dance on the stage with Jim Belushi while somewhere in the Quarter, their men plied the Rev with strippers and lap dances trying to break down his strong will not to transgress. The ladies reached tipsy by the time they arrived at Harrah's to drop some money at the tables and the slots. Okay, a few of them were really drunk. One of the bone-thin super model wives threw up in a waste can and had to be sent home in a taxi. Sharlette called her own cab and filled it with those who needed to leave. Stevie, Mintay and Precious were still on their feet and in their right minds mostly when the patrons of the casino began pointing and whispering, "Sinners!"

The Rev and Calvin Armitage filled most of an entryway. Behind them Connor's blond head and Joe Dean's black hair bobbed. All wore huge shit-eating grins. And why not? Half a dozen barely dressed and overly made up women clung to them like...like, well, like hookers on a John.

"Excuse me, ladies. I got to go kill the father of my children now." Precious strode toward the group of football players and their escorts. She balled up a big fist.

"Precious, baby, they ain't mine." Curse 'Em and Crush 'Em Calvin Armitage tried to remove a redhead who stuck to him as if she had suction cups on her palms. "Don't make me bleed in front of my friends, now, Precious. It's bad for my rep and you know I won't hit you back."

"It's not you I'm gonna hit, Calvin. Get your grip off my man, slut!" She raised a mighty arm above the woman who suddenly released Cal and attached herself to the Rev leaving the groom with two partners.

"That's okay, Cal. You go on home with the little woman and leave the rest for us," Joe Dean told him.

The Rev cordially kissed the hands of both his escorts. "It's been a pleasure, my dears, but I see the woman I'm going home with tonight." Showing no signs of drunkenness, he headed unerringly toward Mintay, bent her over the craps table for a kiss, and said, "Let's get a room for the night, Doc."

Mintay tried for outrage but did not succeed. "How many rooms you been in tonight, huggy bear?"

"None. Those be Joe Dean's women, all of 'em.

They're only arm candy to me. You the woman I love, baby. Let's go across the street and check in so I can prove that to you. All they did was light the fire I keep only for my Mintay."

"Sorry I'm wimping out on you, Stevie. I can't resist this man. See you at the wedding. But you do understand what I mean."

Mintay cocked her head to where Joe Dean and Connor stood with three women each. Two bottle blonde bombshells ran their acrylic nails through Connor's hair. The redhead formed a link to Joe's trio, a slim black woman with a 'fro and a curvaceous Latina with Joe in the middle.

"Come on, man. Three apiece. We can do it. Let's get a suite," Joe Dean urged, oblivious to Stevie's presence.

"No, take your list ladies home, Joe. I see what I want standing right over there."

"Oh shit, it's Stevie Dowd. Pretend I'm not here." Joe turned his entourage of women with the precision of a chorus line and retreated from the casino.

Connor crossed to his intended. "Nothing happened. Joe Dean summoned his next six list ladies and they just latched on to us."

"I believe you, but Mintay is right. We have to get that man married."

****

If sunny days meant happy brides, Dr. Arminta Green had hit the jackpot. The late March afternoon temperatures broiled the overflow guests standing outside the church listening to the service on loudspeakers. Still, Stevie was happy to leave her cramped seat inside, stretch and stand among those waiting for the exit of the bride and groom who had circled round after the recessional to have pictures taken in front of the altar. She searched for a glimpse of the Wish Lady. Ah, there she stood wearing a light green dress with one of those raggedy hems. From the flush on her face, she'd been out in the heat the whole time.

A sack of rice came Stevie's way and she grabbed a big handful before passing it on. The bridal party began to emerge. Stevie dumped half her rice on Mintay and the Rev. She festooned Connor's long, blond hair as he escorted the matron of honor down the steps to the limo and saved some to shower on Joe Dean when he paused to speak to what's her name—Nell. Might be superstitious, but you never knew what would work. Ducking the rice, Joe Dean moved along, but the Wish Lady had vanished like a small, twinkling star into the vast midnight of the Rev's huge kin. Oh well, she'd catch up with her at the reception.

Upon arrival, Stevie found the reception hall jammed with guests who had more sense than to stand outdoors in eighty degree heat and had headed straight for the open bar. She made her way to the reserved tables set aside for close family and friends and put the camera bag she'd brought from the car onto one of the chairs. Now to scope out the Wish Lady. There she was hiding in one of the darker corners.

"Over here, Wish Lady! I have a seat for you." Stevie waved her arm clad in the pearl gray silk outfit Mintay had helped her select. Shod with four inch silver heels, Stevie knew she could not be ignored by her quarry. The Wish Lady drifted her way.

"Mintay asked me to save a place for you and be on the lookout."

Now, all she had to do was engage the little lady in small talk until Joe Dean noticed the one who got away sat right here waiting for him to try again. Stevie got the woman's name straight, asked about her patients, showed her Connor's Super Bowl ring which she wore on a chain around her neck—and then blew it.

"I thought you came to be with Joe Dean, not admire my ring. Oops. I can tell by your expression the bride neglected to mention how she thought a kiddie shrink would be perfect for Joe who is a tad immature. I was supposed to make sure the two of you connected. Sorry."

"A tad—make that a ton. I have no intention of being his number seventy, thanks anyway." Nell started to rise from her specially held seat.

"I believe the man is up to seventy-five now. Really, Joe needs to grow up when it comes to women," Stevie agreed.

Then, their gazes were drawn to where the quarterback stood being photographed with his bridesmaid. He sent a special smile their way and Nell Abbott simply glazed over. So, there was some attraction. Feeling better, Stevie suggested they join the food line. Toasts and dancing followed, but Joe Dean stayed away. The Wish Lady relaxed, plied by an ever full glass of champagne.

Suddenly, the quarterback made his move, swooping up behind Nell like an eagle about to hook a small, green fish. He covered her eyes with his hands and asked, "Guess who?"

How lame was that? And yet, Stevie had to giggle as they bantered back and forth. She'd had quite a bit champagne herself. There, Joe led Nell to the dance floor. The Wish Lady tried to converse; Joe tried to snuggle her against his big chest. Stevie wished Connor would claim her that way. Joe went back to his groomsman duties and the reception continued on and on until Mintay and the Rev left for their "undisclosed honeymoon destination."

Joe materialized as Nell wobbled to her feet and offered her a place to stay for the night since Chapelle had no hotels—his mama's house.

"Go ahead and stay at Joe's place," Stevie urged. "His mama will protect you, guaranteed, as Joe would say."

"Guar-an-teed," Joe repeated with a sparkling grin promising just the opposite. "My Porsche is right out back. We can collect your car tomorrow."

Joe Dean and the Wish Lady left together. Stevie congratulated herself. "And my work here is done."

Chapter Twenty-Five

Stevie Dowd and Connor Riley married at 10:00 a.m. the first Saturday in June before the worst heat of the day in a private lakeshore ceremony performed by Rev Bullock's father. Only best friends and immediate family attended. Stevie held to her very basic instructions for the bridal party—wear something white.

Stevie wore her palest of blue gowns, sleek and yet comfortable. A simple crown of daisies rested on her long, loose hair. Around her neck dangled a large, emerald cut aquamarine and a Super Bowl ring, both on gold chains. The former was a wedding gift from her groom. The latter had been given to her as a token of engagement but was much too large for her to wear on a finger. She refused to have it cut down to her size. For the most part, everyone obeyed her orders for the day. Stevie passed among her guests admiring their outfits and listening to their banter.

Her sister, Michelle, and her mother arrived in lacy tea-length dresses and picture hats fit for a garden party with the queen. Her two nieces, dressed in similar frills, carried wicker baskets full of dried rose petals that when strewn, crunched under the feet of the guests and gave off a sweet, pleasant scent.

At Merrilee's insistence, Colby served as ring bearer. He hated his short white pants and having become very vocal, said so. "Why can't I play with the other kids?"

"Because you are in the wedding, my dear, sweet

boy. Mommy wasn't invited to be matron of honor. Your new Auntie Michelle got that job even though she lives far away in Houston."

Dr. Arminta Green Bullock preferred to get a second use out of her wedding dress. Without the veil, yards long train and choker of diamonds, the gown was really very basic and practical like Mintay herself. Jackie Haile, the third bridesmaid, wore a white satin tuxedo and top hat she'd found in, where else, Las Vegas. Connor and the groomsmen had white dinner jackets custom-made to fit their over large physiques.

Joe Dean called out to Jackie, "Hey, Lesbo, don't I look exactly like James Bond? I bet you can't keep your hands off me."

"You look like a waiter, Jerk," Jackie replied. "But yeah, I can't keep my hands off of you." She bopped him hard, but not in his throwing arm. Joe punched her back, but in a friendly sort of way.

The Rev held up his hands. "Peace! I feel like a waiter in this getup and you don't hear me complaining."

Standing nearby, Kevin Riley wore children's dirty handprints and baby drool on his white coat. Dexter Sykes, who had offered to take the wedding pictures as a truce offering, photographed Kev in all his grungy glory. Now that portrait would be one of her favorite momentos, Stevie was certain. Another image that pleased her in a different way—Kristen Riley, dressed in a white silk suit with a daisy in the buttonhole, her blonde hair in a tasteful chignon, holding her husband's hand and weeping her tears of joy.

Knowing Dex all too well, Stevie insisted on a contract where she got to select the photos that would undoubtedly be sold to every sort of celebrity magazine. Connor and Stevie knew they were destined to be on the cover of *People* again, but Dex did pledge to give the couple a free wedding album.

A reception for four hundred guests awaited the wedding party at the grand old Fairmont Hotel. Amber and Marcello, who had not been invited to the ceremony, told Stevie they would spend their time at the reception profitably by handing out business cards to athletes they thought had modeling and advertising potential. Most likely they would also bore everyone by displaying baby pictures of their newborn, Gabriella Stefania.

Not caring much about the arrangements for the big bash, Stevie left most of the details to Margaret and the very competent staff of the hotel. She and Connor were married with happiness and laughter in the sight of beloved friends and family—all that really mattered.

****

The reception was another matter altogether. The bride and groom stepped from the white stretch limo into a media event insisted upon by Margaret Stutes and the Sinners' PR department. Camera flashes blinded the couple as they raced to the ballroom. Security guards wearing sunglasses to hide their shifting eyes verified each and every guest. The music inside the room ceased and was soon replaced by a drum roll.

"Ladies and gentlemen, let me introduce the bride and groom, Stevie and Connor Riley."

Good, the wedding singer recommended by Precious Armitage had remembered to call her Stevie, not Stephanie, and not Mrs. Connor Riley, as she and her new husband had agreed. He reeled off the names of the rest of the wedding party. Jackie's outfit drew laughter, and the sweet children all dressed in white earned their share of ah's even if they had gotten a little smudged during the marriage process.

Now past noon, Stevie figured they should start the buffet line. Personally, she was starving even if their guests had filled up on hors d'oeuvres and free drinks. She forked up a chilled lobster tail and selected one of the accompanying sauces, ran the gauntlet of tempting side dishes until she reached the rare roast beef being carved at the other end and found she had no room on her plate for the crepes being made to order with a selection of savory fillings or fresh fruit and assorted toppings.

Connor, managing to juggle two plates in his big hands, held out an empty for a crepe stuffed with blueberries and topped by a large dollop of whipped cream. "This is giving me ideas for the wedding night." He kissed her cheek, and Dex set off his flash right in their faces.

"Great shot, Stevie. You are one of the beautiful people now."

She did not feel like one or particularly want to be considered part of that crowd. Too much attention and too little privacy, as far as she was concerned. They dined with four hundred people, few of whom she knew, watching their every bite which made her stomach jitter.

The band cranked up again and immediately, the lead man made a sad error. "The bride will now dance with her father."

What father? She had forgotten to mention Dad was deceased. No one had given her away. They simply stood in front of the Reverend Bullock and got hitched. At the table directly in front of them, her mother dabbed at her eyes and frowned. The crowd parted. Coach Marty Buck, dressed in a tuxedo, claimed her with applause from the audience. Even her mother smiled—and gladly took her place with the coach after Connor cut in taking Stevie in his arms. Kristen and Keith Riley, two people still in love after all these years, joined the dance. Kevin led Merrilee to the floor. The Rev claimed Mintay. Stevie's sister danced with her husband, and Joe Dean—that joker—took Jackie Haile out for a spin. They battled for the lead, dipped each other and brought the house down with their act.

Joe topped that with his James Bond impression performed to draw giggles from three busty blondes who immediately encircled him after his dance. Stevie had no idea who they were or where they came from. Were they some of his list ladies he'd smuggled into the party? Oh, he was going ruin another chance with the Wish Lady if he kept this up.

Unfortunately, Nell had not gone along with the first attempt to pair them and denied Joe after the Rev's wedding. He'd run off to the islands with six of his list ladies to sulk, but she and Mintay agreed to give this match another try. The man was a menace to happily married men.

Stevie scanned the crowd. Where was Nellwyn Abbott? She'd invited that lady at the Rev's wedding and followed up with the engraved invitation. Come on, who could resist an invite to a party like this? Ah, there she was boxed in by the linemen. Her small form stood out in its floaty white dress with its blue floral print. Most of the female guests had elected to wear sophisticated black—mourning the end of Connor's freedom perhaps. Good, Calvin Armitage had seated their special guest at a table with Precious and Sharlette right out front for Joe to see.

Damn, Dex motioned them toward the four-tiered wedding cake. He enjoyed pushing the bride and groom around entirely too much. The pastry chef had done a magnificent job molding pale blue icing with white Swiss dots over the layers and ringing each tier with fresh daisies including the topper. The man hadn't been at all put out by a request for Sinners' red velvet cake on the inside. A groom's cake of dark chocolate formed in the exact shape and size of Connor's jersey with a big, red number eighty in the middle sat to one side. They made the first cut. They nibbled from each other's fingertips, keeping a pact not to do any cake smashing. They toasted with champagne in three different positions and crossed their hands to show off their rings, his a plain broad gold band, hers slim and channeled with diamonds.

Stevie began to relax. Joe Dean had definitely spotted the Wish Lady. Like a shark scenting chum in the water, he neared her table. Seizing a tray of champagne flutes from a passing waiter, he went into action. Pretending to be a server, he played some kind of game with the drinks. Nell did not appear to be playing along.

The band struck up the schmaltzy *When I Fall in Love*. Perfect. Joe lost no time whisking the Wish Lady from her seat and out onto the dance floor. Nell tried to keep up a conversation; Joe kept trying to pull her closer, a repeat performance from the previous wedding. By the end of the song, he managed to tuck Nell Abbott under his chin and tight against his chest. And then, he escorted her back to her seat and left her entirely alone. Double damn.

"Stefania, at last I get you alone. You make the lovely bride. See my *fotografia* of your namesake, my beautiful daughter Gabriella Stefania."

Marcello waved a baby picture—actually more than one—at her. The infant already had a modeling portfolio, had posed for several ads, and her face appeared on a baby food jar, the Italian bragged.

"Yes, she is adorable. Where is Amber?"

"Amber, she floats around seeing if any big football player will sign with us for advertising. Me, I am soliciting the ladies. Too bad you are so old now, but good you get married to a rich man."

"I think you should change that expression to 'inviting the ladies to model' before you get arrested, Marcello."

"Ah, yes. I misuse an American idiom. It is part

of my charm, no?"

Much as Stevie wanted to say no, she agreed with him simply to escape. Where had Joe Dean gone? Kevin had Nell in his clutches on the dance floor. Had their quarterback sneaked out to have an orgy with the three blondes? She would not put it beyond him. Huge Calvin Armitage seized her for a dance and all her attention went toward keeping him off her feet. It wouldn't do to have a limping bride when they made their escape from this chaos. Only one more hour to go.

Finally, time to throw the garter and get rid of the bouquet. Connor drew the pale blue garter, which held up nothing at all, down her long, naked leg. Stevie Dowd hated pantyhose with a passion and what the guys saw drew appreciative hoots from the team. The groom wound up for the throw, and then Joe Dean, obviously roaring drunk, appeared from out of nowhere. How had he gotten so stewed since the last time she saw him? Nell Abbott would not be impressed. The quarterback snagged the lacy elastic band in mid-air and shoved it on his sleeve.

He pointed and said, "No way I'm gonna be the next to marry. Not 'til I hit forty and retire." Joe reeled back into the crush leaving 'em laughing as usual.

The women lined up for the bouquet toss. Nell did not participate even though Sharlette and Precious urged her on. Instead, the clutch of daisies sailed into the hands of Margaret Stutes who had put on some weight in recent months. She wore a loose, animal print shift that only made her look dumpy, unfortunately. But, she did use her new bulk to shove her competition out of the way with the strength of a linebacker. Triumphant, she held the flowers aloft.

"Joe, Joe Dean Billodeaux, where did you go?"

The cry drew cruel laughter. Stevie felt almost sorry for the woman with her pathetic crush on the quarterback. Nothing she could do about it. Her own ordeal was nearly at an end. She congratulated Margaret on her catch and thanked her profusely for all her efforts to make the reception perfect. She announced that the bride and groom wanted to leave and Margaret made it so.

Guests reached for the heaps of poppers shaped like little champagne bottles and the tiny bags of confetti in blue satin sacks embossed with the bride and groom's intertwined initials. They pocketed the silver boxes holding the special chocolates bearing the Sinners' red devil mascot and searched for handbags beneath the pale blue linens draping the tables. Some snatched up the daisy centerpieces as if they were prizes on the midway and stripped the daisy garlands off the pillars and the head table.

Definitely too many daisies in this room. What was left of the flowers were to go to patients in nursing homes; the remaining food to a homeless shelter. The down and out would eat like the rich and famous tonight thanks to Connor Riley.

Stevie and Connor sprinted through the rain of confetti and streamers released by the poppers. Snapping pictures, Dex tailed them to the limo for one last shot.

"Good luck with this one, Stevie. I gotta go. Heard a rumor Joe Dean is reeling drunk and picked up a teenager to take back to his place."

Steve paused as she bent to get into the vehicle. "Joe wouldn't do that. He'd never date anyone that young. It's against what principles he has."

"See the proof in next week's tabloids. Bon voyage, baby."

Dex took off running to his next opportunity. Stevie settled in beside Connor and rested her head on his broad shoulder.

"Joe wouldn't, would he?" she asked her new husband.

"I don't think so. He's still trying to get over that

nightmare evening with Margaret Stutes after the Super Bowl. I didn't think he'd ever get that drunk again."

"Oh, I get it. Joe finally hooked up with the Wish Lady. She does look kind of young. What a relief."

Connor told the driver to get going. They headed for the airport with a string of paparazzi in pursuit. Having alerted the security people in advance, the celebrities raced through the metal detectors and claimed their small carry-ons with a minimum of delay. They split from each other at the restrooms and reappeared dressed like normal people, Stevie in jeans, T-shirt and ball cap, Connor wearing all black and his Sinners' jacket. They made a U-turn and slipped back into the main body of the airport. Their limo still waited at the curb to take them back to the house on the lakeside.

****

Connor waited for his bride in the hot tub. Rose petals from the wedding ceremony still floated on the surface of the water. They'd made love once in the comfort of their own bed, but now the sun had gone down. The air and water matched temperatures. The stars shone overhead, winking in the humid night. Wrapped in only a white towel, Stevie came to him moving across the darkened deck. She flung the towel away, no sagging swimsuits or trunks between them now.

She settled her back on top of his broad chest and bent her head to nestle under his chin. He kissed the top of her hair and reached around to stroke her breasts with both hands. His erection popped up between her legs. She laughed and reached to touch him. No need to rush, no urgency now.

"I'm glad we decided to come back here where it all started. The islands can wait another day." She looked up at the stars and enjoyed the touch of his strong fingers.

"Me, too. It would be a shame to leave behind that big bowl of chocolate mousse Miss Essie put in the refrigerator. We can use it up later tonight. But our love did not start here."

"Well, I doubt if they would let us in the Super Dome so we could do it on the sidelines this time of night."

"Farther back, the day I sacked you into that pile of leaves at my parents' house."

"Not for me. I took a little longer. Thanks for waiting. I wonder if Joe Dean will ever know how to love like this. I tried my best to fix him up with the Wish Lady today, but he probably threw away that chance again by getting drunk."

"You know what? Joe Dean Billodeaux is the last person I want to think about on my wedding night. He's on his own right now."

"Maybe, maybe not."

Stevie stopped teasing him and turned over. She took in his fullness and moved slowly up and down. Connor closed his eyes and enjoyed. But before he lost himself in her completely, he wanted to tell his bride one more thing.

"Stevie, you know what we got—it *is* a joy forever."

Epilogue

Connor Riley played football for the New Orleans Sinners three more years. During that time, the Sinners took two Super Bowls. A severe knee injury in his last year of play told Riley the time to quit had come. He went on to football commentating during the season but became better known as a motivational speaker. He delivered the message of how to overcome fear with the help of friends and loved ones.

Retirement blessed the Rileys with other rewards. Nine months after his last game, Stevie gave birth to their first child. Keeping her promise to Jackie, she christened him Jack Haile Riley. Eighteen months later, a second child was born to the Rileys. Joe Dean Billodeaux demanded to be named godfather to this one. He claimed as he held tiny Josee Deana Riley near the baptismal font, she had batted her long lashes over her big, blue eyes and given him a very sexy, toothless smile.

At the age of forty, Stevie mistook a third pregnancy for early menopause. She could no longer avoid naming a child after Rev Bullock who reminded the Rileys often that his twins, Connor and Riley, and his youngest boy, Little Joe, were already in grade school. Still, he did not have his own namesake. Unable to foist the name Revelation Jeremiah on any helpless child, Stevie created one of her own, Arjay Bullock Riley. The Rev approved. Retiring the season after Connor, he gave as his reasons a desire to serve the Lord and to spend more time with his family. Now, he had plenty of years to shape little Arjay into the football player he would become.

Merrilee, not to be outdone, gave birth to two more children, each born three months after Stevie's babies. She named them Kelly and Keegan. Her last child arrived the year she turned forty-one, nine months after discovering Kevin kept a mistress in the French Quarter. The boy bore the name Quade Michael, but the family called him Quits. She continued to claim she was the better mother because Stevie had elected not to nurse. Because of Merrilee's religious convictions, Kevin never, ever got a divorce.

Jackie Haile, who became known fondly to the Riley children as Uncle Jackie, gave the toddling Jack his first set of plastic golf clubs. Immediately upon finishing college with the business degree insisted upon by his parents, he joined the pro golf circuit where he succeeded brilliantly managed by his Uncle Jackie. The media dubbed him the White Tiger Woods. Within a year, he became known as simply the White Tiger for his blond good looks. Golf being so much safer than football, his career decision made his mother joyous.

At the age of sixteen Josee Riley, who had inherited a golden beauty and even longer legs than Stevie, was offered a modeling contract by the Amberello Agency. Stevie absolutely forbid this. Sometimes, having Joe Dean as a *parrain,* a French godfather, paid off. He told her to ask her mother about the photos she had posed for wearing only sand, and he knew where her dad kept the posters, too. This made up for all the years of being dragged to sporting events and enduring the chronic joke about everyone standing up for her at a game and asking, "Josee, can you see?" As a small child, she had actually believed this.

At the age of twenty-one, Josee Riley posed for a *Sports Illustrated* swimsuit issue. Photographed by, according to her, a gross, balding old lech named Dexter Sykes who claimed to have known her mother rather well, Josee gave up modeling for more serious pursuits.

As for Joe Dean Billodeaux, he quarterbacked until the age of forty, just as he said he would, and retired with five Super Bowl rings. Afterward, the Amberello Agency arranged several lucrative advertising and minor acting stints for him based mainly on his handsome, craggy face, but he preferred being at home on his ranch in Chapelle, Louisiana. Believe it or not, Joe Dean eventually did learn there was more to life than sex and football.

Joe Dean's story is told in the sequel *Wish for a Sinner.*

www.ingramcontent.com/pod-product-compliance
Lightning Source LLC
LaVergne TN
LVHW050627100826
845148LV00011B/1766

* 9 7 8 1 6 0 1 5 4 7 1 7 0 *